MATTHEW SWANSON & ROBBI BEHR

the Real McCoys

WONDER UNDER COVER

[Imprint]
MAKE YOUR MARK

NEW YORK

To Erin, who already has all the badges.

Special thanks to Yudhijit Bhattacharjee, Brenda Chen, Mario Manzoli, Mandira Mehra Parsh, Mohammed Mobaidin, Christian Vainieri, and Elena Wimpy for fact checking the language translations—and to Jonna Hamilton for helping us make sure Moxie's mom would not be mocked by other scientists.

[Imprint]
MAKE YOUR MARK

A part of Macmillan Publishing Group, LLC
120 Broadway, New York, NY 10271

THE REAL MCCOYS: WONDER UNDERCOVER. Text copyright © 2019 by
Matthew Swanson. Illustrations copyright © 2019 by Robbi Behr. All rights reserved.
Printed in the United States of America by LSC Communications, Harrisonburg, Virginia.

Library of Congress Cataloging-in-Publication Data

Names: Swanson, Matthew, 1974-author. | Behr, Robbi, illustrator.
Title: The Real McCoys: Wonder Undercover / Matthew Swanson ; Robbi Behr.
Other titles: Wonder undercover
Description: First edition. | New York : Imprint, 2019. | Summary:
Fourth-grade detective Moxie McCoy joins the Wonder Scouts as she and her little brother, Milton, in-
vestigate how one Dublinger twin is sabotaging the other in the race to earn the most badges. Identifiers:
LCCN 2019002535 | ISBN 9781250307828 (hardcover) Subjects: | CYAC: Mystery and detective stories.
| Brothers and sisters—Fiction. | Detectives—Fiction. | Scouting (Youth activity)—Fiction. | Twins—
Fiction. | Schools—Fiction.
Classification: LCC PZ7.S9719 Rem 2019 | DDC [Fic]—dc23
LC record available at https://lccn.loc.gov/2019002535

Our books may be purchased in bulk for promotional, educational, or business use. Please contact your
local bookseller or the Macmillan Corporate and Premium Sales Department at (800) 221-7945 ext. 5442
or by e-mail at MacmillanSpecialMarkets@macmillan.com.

Book design by Robbi Behr and Natalie C. Sousa

Imprint logo designed by Amanda Spielman

First edition, 2019

10 9 8 7 6 5 4 3 2 1

mackids.com

Welcome, dear reader. Please stay for a while
As Moxie and Milton solve problems in style.
Read, laugh, and wonder, but when you are finished,
Don't hide it away or its fate is diminished.
Books are for sharing. Stories will bind us.
(But stuck on your bookshelf, no one will find us.)

CHAPTER 1: DUBLINGER DISCORD

The name's Moxie. Moxie McCoy.

The world's greatest fourth-grade detective, at your service.

Here I am, 20 minutes before school starts, standing behind an extremely large bush.

WHY?

Because Emily Estevez, my very best friend in the whole entire world, asked me to.

It is a sneaky place to stand, and I like it.

Emily appears with a look that means she has terrible news or has recently had too much

"What did you have for breakfast?" I ask.

"Toast and jam."

"What's the bad news?"

"The truth is, I have very *good* news." But Emily says *good* the way a doctor says, *"Don't worry— this won't hurt a bit,"* right before jamming a

NEEDLE

into your arm. "Please try to keep an open mind," Emily says.

"I always do!"

"You sometimes don't."

I am tempted to feel wounded, but since I am talking to Emily, good as cheesecake, pure as water from the door of the refrigerator, I decide to keep an open mind. Emily has never led me astray.

I will try.

Good. The truth is, I have a case for you. But the name of your new client might . . . surprise you.

I have traveled the wide world. I have been to New Jersey. Which is to say, *nothing* surprises me.

Emily glances over my shoulder and gives a nod. I turn and see one unlovable Dublinger lurking behind a different bush nearby.

> The Dublinger twins, Tammy and Tracy, are my sworn enemies.

Tracy is

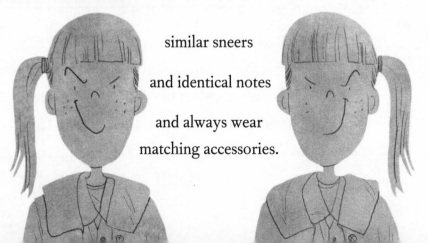

QUEEN OF THINGS THAT ARE AWFUL AND IRRITATING,

and Tammy is the jester in her court.

At the moment, I can't tell which Dublinger I'm looking at, because they have

similar sneers

and identical notes

and always wear matching accessories.

The Dublinger approaches. I am preparing to say

 or  or

But Emily speaks first. "Hello, Tammy. Moxie has agreed to hear about your case and . . . *to keep an open mind.*"

Hello, Tammy, I say with about as much pleasure as I might get from kissing a clam.

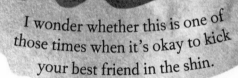

I wonder whether this is one of those times when it's okay to kick your best friend in the shin.

Tammy gnaws at the center of my soul with her beady blue termite-teeth eyes.

What seems to be the problem?

asks Milton, surprising me a little.

If I forgot to mention that my puny little brother, Milton, has been standing beside me this whole time, it's because he's so short that it almost hurts my neck to look down that far.

4

Milton fancies himself a detective, and technically we're partners, so I let him tag along when I'm working on cases. He sometimes says useful things. But mostly he collects dust and resembles a miniature accountant.

"Well?" I ask, tapping my foot to make perfectly clear how little patience I have left.

"It's better if I show you," says Tammy, who looks as if she'd rather tickle a triceratops than talk to me.

She pulls back her coat and reveals . . . her

WONDER SCOUTS SASH.

Ugh, I say before I can stop myself. And then, even though I could definitely stop myself, I say it again.

UGH.

5

The Wonder Scouts is a group of girls who think they are better than every other person on the planet. They wear blue sashes loaded with

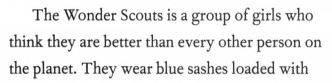

MEANINGLESS BADGES

They spend at least two hours a day combing their hair. They meet three times a week to come up with new ways to be awful.

They have always made me think of Annabelle Adams, Girl Detective, Volume 23:

Not-So-Nice Guys,

in which a group of seemingly pleasant and charitable citizens turns out to be a renegade band of no-good swindlers who help little old ladies cross the street but then steal their purses and use the money to send fragile toys filled with glitter to unsuspecting toddlers.

But despite all that is wrong with the Wonder Scouts,
I can't help but be enchanted by Tammy's blue sash.
It is a magnificent mosaic of colorful patches, each a
delicately embroidered
reminder of accomplishment.

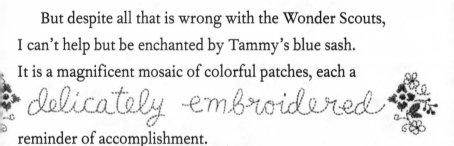

"So . . ." says Milton, trying to get us
back on track, "what seems to be the *problem*?"

Tammy Dublinger points to the one empty
spot on her sash.

the
MASTER
BAKER
BADGE

It's the last one I need to become the first Wonder Scout
to get all twenty badges. And I can't seem to do it.

"Nobody's perfect," says Milton in a comforting way.
"I am!" says Tammy in an irritating way.

Apparently not,

I say, looking at Tammy the way
you look at a swarm of gnats
before pulling out your bug spray.

"Maybe not *perfect*, but I *absolutely* know how to mix up a perfect meringue. And yet every time I've tried during a badge challenge, something has gone MYSTERIOUSLY wrong."

"Do you want us to teach you how to make meringue?" asks Milton. "I might be able to find a recipe online."

"NO!" says Tammy. "I make *perfect* meringue at home. The only thing standing between me and the Master Baker badge is Tracy. I know she is sabotaging me. I just don't know how."

Suddenly, this case has my undivided attention. If Tammy is a rainy day that ruins your picnic, Tracy is a full-blown hurricane that flattens your pony-themed birthday party.

One Dublinger is hiring me to bring about the downfall of the other. This is the most wonderful thing since the invention of the book.

"I got my nineteenth badge a *month* ago. At that point, Tracy had only *fourteen*. Now she has nineteen badges, too. Now *she* could become the first Wonder Scout to get all twenty badges! Which would be *unacceptable!*" Tammy is getting pretty worked up. It's really kind of wonderful.

"What, exactly, do you want us to do?" I ask.

"Figure out what Tracy is doing to keep me from winning this badge. Expose her as the sneaky, lying cheater she is!" Tammy pulls a dollar from her pocket. "Will you take my case?" she asks, suddenly reluctant, as if asking a giraffe to lick her earlobe.

Milton and I lock eyes.

The challenge is clear, but the answer is *Oh heck yes.* We've been looking for the next big case. And this one is

the REAL McCOY.

CHAPTER 2: TIDDLYWHUMP'S FINEST

The next morning at breakfast, Milton is reading the newspaper. Not *A First Grader's Book About Puppies*. Not *Jim and Jen Eat Jam*. The actual *newspaper*.

Look at this,

he says.

I do not want to look. I am busy thinking about meringue, that delightful fluffy substance that lives atop my seventh-favorite kind of pie.

Look!

he insists.

I glance in the tiniest, barely-est way so I can say I looked and Milton will have to be quiet.

Someone broke into the Local House of History last night!

This is **SHOCKING!**

The **LOCAL HOUSE OF HISTORY** is a source of pride for all Tiddlywhumpians. Breaking into the Local House of History is like kicking a duckling.

QUACK!

"What happened?" I ask.

"It says the Chief Historian was working late when he heard a loud crash from the basement. He called the police, but by the time they arrived, the intruder had disappeared."

A horrible thought occurs to me. "Is Columbus okay?"

It was on my second-grade field trip that I first encountered the bronze statue of Columbus, an extremely noble pig who once saved town founder (and notoriously heavy sleeper), Marcus Tiddlywhump, from certain peril by dragging him by the leg of his pajamas to the safety of the cyclone cellar as a tornado approached.

11

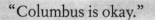

"Columbus is okay."

"*Whew!* What was stolen?"

"That's just the thing! Nothing seems to be missing!" Milton looks appropriately baffled.

"That sounds fishy."

"I agree." Milton looks appropriately suspicious.

"Does it mention any clues?"

"Just that a basement window was left ajar."

"Who is the lead detective? Wait. Don't tell me. Is it Multani?"

"It's Multani."

"He's Tiddlywhump's finest."

"That's what they say."

Detective Multani cracked the CASE OF THE CLATTERING CONVERTIBLE,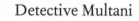

unraveled the Mystery OF THE MOLDY MAUSOLEUM

and exposed the THOROUGHLY UNLAWFUL MANEUVERINGS OF THE TIDDLYWHUMP SEVEN.

If Multani is on the case, I consider it as good as solved.

But Milton looks worried. "Why would someone break in and not take anything? It doesn't make sense."

I am tempted to remind Milton that criminals often *don't* make a lick of sense, as in Annabelle Adams, Girl Detective, Volume 49: *Cause and No Effect,* in which a notorious criminal mastermind spends seven years plotting to crack the unbreakable vault in the

LABYRINTH OF UNTHINKABLE COMPLEXITY

and, when he finally succeeds, steals only a plastic mood ring, leaving the great mound of rubies and diamonds untouched.

As far as I know, there are no rubies or diamonds at the Local House of History. Its noble offerings feature mostly just photos and colonial knickknacks. And Columbus, of course.

"Come on," I say. "It's time for school."

But Milton's eyes are still glued to the article, drilling for information that does not seem to be there.

13

Later at school, my teacher, Mr. Shine, sits on the edge of his desk, like he always does, asking us questions instead of teaching us things.

I like Mr. Shine, and his class is loads of fun, but I wonder what will happen when I get to fifth grade and I haven't learned any of the stuff fourth graders are supposed to know.

Instead of thinking hard about the many important differences between similes and metaphors, I am pondering my new case, which is made all the more delicious by the fact that my client is sitting to MY RIGHT and my primary suspect is sitting to MY LEFT.

Both Dublingers are making faces like the sky before a thunderstorm, which is not unusual, but today they are looking right past me and shooting lightning bolts at each other instead.

At first recess, I find Milton at our bench, where, on a normal day, our detective agency,  would meet with clients and discuss ongoing cases. But since we are 100% focused on our *new* case, we tell the long line of kids to get lost, and we talk to Emily instead.

Emily is not *officially* part of our agency, because the pressures of detective work give her gas, but she is SMART and full of GOOD IDEAS and always willing to help us think through puzzles when we're stuck.

Here's the problem, I say.

I don't want to get within twenty feet of a Wonder Scout. But I cannot solve this case without getting *extremely close* to a whole roomful of them.

5'   10'

I think of Annabelle Adams, Girl Detective, Volume 43: *No Me Gusta,*

"¡PERO ME ENCANTAN LOS CIANOTIPOS, MAMÁ!"

in which Annabelle poses as the long-lost daughter of the famously irritating Señora Conchita de Albondiga to get her hands on the secret blueprints to the GRANDE GRAN SECRETO ALBATROS MECÁNICOS de CARAMELO.

To pull it off, she learns Spanish, dyes her hair to match the Señora's, and pretends to enjoy petting extremely small dogs.

I suddenly know what must be done.

"What do you mean?" asks Emily.

"I must infiltrate their ranks! I must learn their secrets!" I pace like a detective does, back and forth, head down, hands jammed deep in my pockets, a look of intense discomfort on my face.

There is no alternative. I must go *undercover*!

Emily makes a face of concern. Milton gives a shriek of delight.

"Yes!" he says. His eyes grow wide as he contemplates the possibilities. "You'll need to *look* like a Wonder Scout."

But . . . what does a Wonder Scout look like? asks Emily.

 Like a conniving, underhanded Dublinger!

That's not exactly what I meant.

You'll need to *act* like a Wonder Scout!

How does a Wonder Scout act?

Like a backstabbing, sister-betraying Dublinger.

Emily gives me a disapproving look. "Wait," she says, "I have an idea." She walks over and starts to chat with a girl I don't recognize.

 Who's that? I ask Milton.

 Henrietta Bork. She's in fifth grade.

 Really? I swear I've never seen her before in my life.

Henrietta ambles over about as swiftly as a tortoise with a leg cramp.

18

"So . . . Henrietta," says Emily, "Moxie is curious about Wonder Scouts. What can you tell us?"

Henrietta shuffles her feet and gives us a few good "uhms" before saying,

Wonder Scouts is an organization devoted to the education and empowerment of optimistic young women through activities and experiences that promote strong values, bolster inner fortitude, and invigorate the spirit. Only young women of sterling character may join.

The words roll off Henrietta's tongue as if she has spent long hours practicing them in front of a haunted mirror while it slowly devoured important pieces of her soul. The three of us stand there, a little bit stunned.

"Thanks, Henrietta," says Emily.

No problem,

says Henrietta as the tide carries her slowly back to sea.

"'Optimistic young women' . . . of 'sterling character,'" I repeat. "It sounds like I'll need to look . . . I don't know . . . **WHOLESOME?**"

"Impossible," says Milton.

"Here," says Emily.

She removes the rubber bands from my pigtails,

takes off her headband to put it on my head,

and pushes my hair around before smiling and saying,

Not bad at all.

I peer into the tiny mirror I always carry in case I need to signal a rescue helicopter. I look like a ten-year-old preschool teacher.

No, I say. Because, *no*.

It's perfect! says Milton.

No way!

I may be a detective, but I have my principles.

"It's what *Annabelle* would do," says Milton, making the one argument he knows will always get my attention.

 Of course, he's right.

And Annabelle wouldn't stop with just a preschool teacher hairdo. She'd put on preschool teacher clothes and learn preschool songs and eat nothing but preschool teacher meals for a full week to cultivate convincing preschool teacher breath.

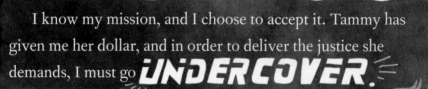

I know my mission, and I choose to accept it. Tammy has given me her dollar, and in order to deliver the justice she demands, I must go **UNDERCOVER.**

And, I think, *by infiltrating the Wonder Scouts, I will gain access to the top secret knowledge needed to bring an end to the evil organization once and for all!* Future generations will thank me for my noble deeds. It is possible that someone will carve a statue of me—but hopefully with my regular hairdo and not my undercover-preschool-teacher look.

21

"Fine," I say. "I'll do it."

Milton and Emily seem pleased.

"But . . . you need to come with me," I say to Emily.

I'm a lot worried about what might happen when I am left by myself with all those Wonder Scouts. I could be eaten alive. Or, worse, forced to hug a Dublinger.

But Emily is not wearing the face I hoped to see. "Sorry. I gave Wonder Scouts a try last year and decided it's not for me."

"You *did*?" I am shocked, as if Emily just admitted to having a secret sister named *Linda*.

"Henrietta asked me to join. I went to a few meetings."

"Why did you quit?"

"Organized group activities give me GAS."

I wonder whether Emily needs to see a doctor to discuss her questionable *intestines*, but mostly I'm relieved that, despite being the nicest person I know, Emily shares my opinion of Wonder Scouts.

I turn to Milton. "I guess it's you and me, *partner*."

Milton has spent a lot of time insisting I call him my detective *partner*, and I am delighted to have a chance to use it against him.

He turns the color of an Oreo's insides and gives me a look that says,

Wonder Scouts is just for girls!

I give him a look that says,

But this is your golden opportunity to break new ground by becoming the first-ever boy Wonder Scout.

He gives me a look that says,

Thanks, but I'm pretty sure the Dublingers would not be okay with that plan.

I give him a look that says,

It was worth a try, wasn't it?

He gives me a look that says,

I guess so, but can we get back to the matter at hand?

"What are you guys *doing*?" asks Emily, who apparently needs to hear actual words to understand what we're saying.

"Milton and I have decided that I will be the *lead detective* on this particular case."

"And that I will offer *logistical support*," Milton chimes in. Which is just his fancy way of saying that he will sit around eating cupcakes and crackers while I do all the hard work and that he will take the clues I collect and spin them around in his great big blender of a brain until a theory pops out.

Apparently, Milton is not done. "And *I* will continue to monitor the developing situation at

"The Local House of History! *What happened?*" demands Emily, who loves local history almost as much as Milton does.

THE LOCAL HOUSE OF HISTORY

Milton tells Emily about the break-in.

Is Columbus okay?

she asks with a gasp.

He is.

Whew. Is Multani on the case?

Yes. He's Tiddlywhump's finest, you know.

That's what they say.

I leave Milton and Emily to their chatter. Because I am confident that Detective Multani will have caught the culprit by the time we get home from school, I turn my full attention to the Case of the Treacherous Twin.

I glance over at the Dublingers, who are playing tetherball with about as much joy as dolphins on a flying trapeze. I study their movements, their facial expressions, their impeccable ponytails. It will take more than a headband to complete my transformation from the *Magnificence* OF M^cCOY TO THE WICKEDNESS OF *Wonder*.

CHAPTER 3: THE FIRST MEETING

During first recess on Wednesday, I inform the crowd of eager kids that M&M, Inc., will be closed indefinitely while we focus on a case so important that it could shape the future of Tiddlywhump and beyond.

While our would-be clients wander off sadly, Emily, Milton, and I discuss my disguise.

Emily has brought the perfect headband, a shade of blue that exactly matches the Wonder Scout sash.

I tell them my plan to wear the bright pink flower girl dress I wore for my aunt Donna's wedding.

Of course, I loathe dresses and probably would have gotten rid of it ages ago, but Mom told me not to in case Aunt Donna gets married more than once.

And then we turn to establishing my character.

I start with the basics.

When Annabelle goes undercover, she always uses an accent.

What kind of accent do Wonder Scouts use?

asks Milton.

I have no idea,

I admit.

"Do I need to get Henrietta?" asks Emily.

"Who?"

Emily points to a girl I swear I've never seen before in my life. "We talked to her *yesterday*!" says Emily, who usually doesn't get so exasperated.

Suddenly, I remember.

No! Henrietta talks like a sleepy robot,

I say, doing my best sleepy-robot impression.

Milton takes a different approach.

Which accents do you know?

The question raises a problem. Since Annabelle lives inside a book, I'm only familiar with what the various accents are *called*. I'm not sure how they sound.

But Emily and Milton don't know that.

British,

Spanish,

Upper Barmonian,

Lower Barmonian,

feisty french Housekeeper,

Irritated Peruvian Pirate,

Sleepy German Baroness with Lingering Heartburn . . .

I could go on.

I'm *guessing* Wonder Scouts have a private way of speaking that they don't reveal until they're sure no one else is listening. I'll just have to wait and see what it sounds like and then do my best to talk that way.

"Makes sense," says Emily.

"Sounds difficult," says Milton.

"Difficult is my middle name," I say. Of course, this is not true. But, gosh, I wish it were.

The rest of the school day goes by, and I can't learn a thing. My brain is already full, like a chef at the end of a

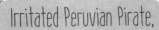

COOKIE CONVENTION.

That night, Dad drives me to my first Wonder Scouts meeting, in the basement of the Tiddlywhump Community Center.

"What's with the party dress?" he asks, failing to hide his surprise.

"This is an extremely fancy club."

"And the glasses?"

To complete my disguise, I have added a pair of rhinestone-encrusted spectacles from the costume box.

And a pair of fancy white gloves.

"You're always telling Milton and me to express our originality. Would you agree that I look extremely *original*?"

"Without a doubt. So, what's this club?"

"The Wonder Scouts. It's for young women of *sterling* character." I smile with all my teeth, letting Dad see just how sterling I am.

29

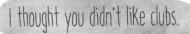

I thought you didn't like clubs.

I have often told Dad that I am far too original to join a club.

That may be true, but you and Mom always tell me to keep an open mind.

That's very wise, says Dad, laughing a little.

There's nothing dads like more than hearing you say their wise words back to them.

Just like you. And it's the truest thing I've said all day. I've never met a smarter, kinder, wiser person than Dad.

Unless it's Mom.

But at the moment, Mom is in a tiny purple submarine, bravely scouring a deep-sea trench off the northeast coast of New Zealand in search of supergiant amphipods, which are sometimes called the insects of the sea. This is very exciting for Mom, but pretty hard for all of us, since cell phones don't work underwater.

When we pull up to the curb, Tammy and Tracy are already lurking by the front door. I get out of the car, and they give me a

DOUBLE GLARE.

If Tammy is happy to see me, she's doing her best to keep it to herself.

I go inside. There in the meeting room is my classmate Megan Lacey, who always wears lime-green nail polish. Megan is only slightly more lovable than the Dublingers. The thought of talking to her makes me

But I have a case to solve. And so I take a deep breath and harness my inner Annabelle.

BLINK BLINK BLINK BLINK B

"*Meg*an," I say, smiling and batting my eyelashes as if I were greeting a minor celebrity.

"*Mox*ie," says Megan, as if I were a piece of ham she forgot to take out of her lunch box on Friday afternoon, and now it's Monday morning.

"What's with the fancy dress?" Megan knows me as someone who tends to err on the side of casual.

"What . . . *this old thing*? It's just something I slip into when I'm feeling particularly . . . *wholesome*. So, what are you doing here?"

I'm afraid I can't tell you.

Megan puts her hands across her sash as if it were

A CUPBOARD FULL OF secrets

"It's okay, Megan. I'm here to join the Wonder Scouts."

Megan looks at me with horror. "You can't! You have to be nominated."

"Excellent. I assume *you'll* nominate me. We're old friends, you and I." Annabelle has taught me that the best way to make someone believe you're *their* friend is to tell them they're *your* friend.

"We *are?*"

"Of course. Remember that time on the playground?"

Megan looks confused, which makes sense. There was no "time on the playground."

"You have to *earn* your nomination," she insists.

"Great. How?"

"By being *worthy*."

I scoff.

If there is anyone more worthy than Moxie McCoy, I'd be afraid to meet her.

I am about to explain the eleven ways in which I'm worthy, when a tall, stern, noble-looking woman strides into the room like the queen of all lions.

She is POWERFUL. She is *Elegant*. I might even call her MAGNIFICENT. Without knowing why, I want her to like me.

33

I join the other girls as we form a circle.

Good evening, Wonder Scouts. Before we get started, I see a new face in our midst.

Step forward, young woman.

I step forward.

Chin up. Back straight!

I raise my chin and straighten my back and wonder if this is how mannequins feel when they are modeling a trendy new blazer.

Who is your sponsor?

Excuse me?

Wonder Scouts is a group of young women of remarkable promise and unimpeachable ethics. We are wary of inviting anyone into our midst without a character reference. Is there anyone here who can vouch for . . . .

What is your name?

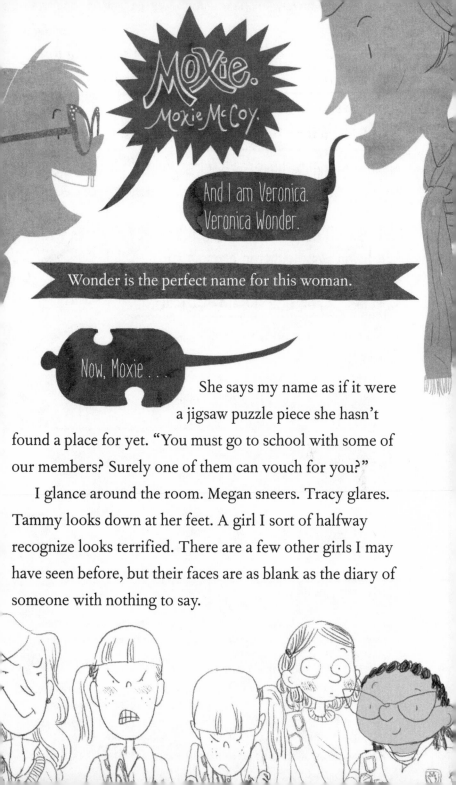

MoXie.

MoXie McCoy.

And I am Veronica. Veronica Wonder.

Wonder is the perfect name for this woman.

Now, Moxie . . .

She says my name as if it were a jigsaw puzzle piece she hasn't found a place for yet. "You must go to school with some of our members? Surely one of them can vouch for you?"

I glance around the room. Megan sneers. Tracy glares. Tammy looks down at her feet. A girl I sort of halfway recognize looks terrified. There are a few other girls I may have seen before, but their faces are as blank as the diary of someone with nothing to say.

Veronica peers deep into my eyes, as if searching for secrets of the universe. "Well then. Please tell me why you think you should be a Wonder Scout."

I chew on that. It's probably not the best idea to say,

I am trying to help my sworn enemy defeat my other sworn enemy while gaining the knowledge necessary to bring your sinister organization **TO ITS KNEES!**

So I say other things instead.

Because I am strong

and swift

and smart

and fearless

and swashbuckling

and—

"That's enough, thank you," says Veronica. "I admire your self-confidence. But what about humility?"

I have heard the word, but I don't *entirely* know what it means.

"What about it?"

"*Humility* is an awareness of one's shortcomings. What are your shortcomings, Moxie?"

It's as if she has asked me to explain why $2 + 2 = 5$

"I pride myself on doing the right thing 100% of the time. I am *allergic* to shortcomings."

"Are you saying you're *perfect*?"

"Of course not. Nobody's *Perfect*."

"Well, then . . . ?"

I search wildly for shortcomings but am drawing a blank.

"Let's see . . . I can't fly a helicopter. Not yet, anyway."

"Okay. What else?"

"I've never won a Nobel Prize."

A girl with curly dark hair and sassy red glasses steps forward. I've never seen her before. She has a GLEAM in her eye.

"I nominate Moxie!"

Veronica looks surprised. "On what are you basing your nomination, Hilly?"

"I like how she talks."

"Very well," says Veronica. "Does anyone *second* the nomination?"

I am standing in a circle of mice.

After a long pause, Tammy Dublinger raises her hand. It seems she has *finally* realized that I'm here to work on *her* case.

I second the nomination.

Tracy glares at her sister as if Tammy just slapped her in the face with a *cold, wet glove!*

"On what are you basing your nomination, Tammy?"

I watch as Tammy's brain searches for a way to justify her outrageous act of Dublinger betrayal.

YES!

I like her ridiculous outfit.

Suddenly, Tracy gets the joke and gives Tammy the meanest high five in the history of evil-twin celebratory hand slaps. A couple of the other girls snicker for a moment until Veronica gives them a glare that shuts them right up.

"All right, then," says Veronica. "As I'm sure you know, Moxie, Wonder Scouts is an organization built on

SISTERHOOD *AND* TRUST

Do you promise to keep our secrets?"

Veronica looks at me like she's sequencing my DNA and washing my hair at the same time.

I had not *intended* to keep any Wonder Scout secrets, but I suppose I could be persuaded to do so, especially since my *actual* mission is securing the downfall of a Dublinger. "I do," I say. "I promise."

Veronica's eyes relax into a smile. "Very well, then. Welcome to the Wonder Scouts. You have earned your first badge."

She hands me an embroidered patch that shows a hand with three fingers raised in the shape of a W. And I find myself loving it despite every awful thing it represents.

Veronica lifts her three middle fingers in the air and holds them out toward me. I do the same, and our fingertips touch, and I feel like I grow an inch instantly.

WOO HOO!

BRAVO!

CHEERS!

YESS!

HOORAY!

L RIGHT!

YAY!

EAH!

Everyone cheers with the exception of Tracy and Tammy, who scowl like vampires sitting by a plate of garlic knots.

> Here is your sash. Wear it with pride.

Veronica hands me a satiny loop of blue cloth. I know the sash represents everything that is wrong with the Wonder Scouts, but I cannot resist its undeniable allure.

> Here is your compass. Learn to use it and you will never find yourself lost.

Until this moment, I had no idea how much I have always wanted a compass.

> Here is your guidebook. Study it well. In the back is a list of all the badges you can earn as a Wonder Scout. Think of it as twenty ways to learn and grow.

> And now let's get this meeting started, shall we?

Without further prompting, every girl stands at attention, opens her mouth, and starts to sing:

I am a Wonder Scout, swift, strong, and smart.
Fearless and loyal and bursting with heart.
When the going gets tough, I power right through it.
When something needs doing, I step up and do it.

There are various hand motions and dance moves. I had no idea this case was going to involve jazz hands.

My skills, they are many. My wisdom is endless.
Never again shall I find myself friendless.
Whatever the trouble, we aim to defeat it.
No matter the challenge, Wonder can meet it.

It's an exciting song with a good tune. In spite of myself, I'm tapping my toes and wishing I knew the words.

The girl with the glasses winks at me.

I'll teach you later,

she whispers.

I start to thank her, but Veronica Wonder is already moving on.

And now for the Credo. It's on PAGE TWO of your guidebook, Moxie.

As I open my book and turn to page two, every girl stands and speaks as one.

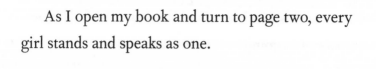

1. You don't need to be proper or quiet or sweet. You need to be you.

2. But never be mean. Especially to other girls.

3. Do not aspire to be normal. It is the opposite of interesting.

4. Never try to dig a hole with a saw or to cut a board with a shovel.

5. The easiest route is not always shortest. The shortest route is not always best.

6. *You are capable of astonishing things.*

7. *Be willing to admit when you're wrong.*

8. *You have the power to change your own story.*

9. *Always, always remember where you came from.*

10. *Experience is your greatest treasure.*

As I stand there with the guidebook in my hands, I realize that I have been handed the secret blueprints to the

TOWERING SKYSCRAPER OF CALAMITY

that is the Wonder Scouts. But I hardly have time to look for clues and plot the Scouts' downfall before Veronica is off on a new topic.

Tonight's lesson is about soap.

I'm not sure I heard her correctly, but it sounds as if we're going to learn about soap. Veronica continues.

Soap has shaped the course of human history.

I suddenly confirm that my precious time is being wasted on

SOAP.

Soap is not exciting and wonderful. Soap is not daring and bold. Soap is for cleaning socks. And scrubbing plates. And washing underwear. Soap is . . . *soap*.

I consider abandoning my mission and running for the hills, but Veronica seems so genuinely excited about soap that I can't help but give her the benefit of the doubt. Over the next half hour, she proceeds to tell us about how long-ago prairie women used to make soap by combining

 (a goopy, greasy mess) and

(a toxic, chemically disaster) over a

When I was trekking in southern Siberia one summer, I saved a little girl who had been cornered by a pair of steppe wolves.

"To thank me, her family threw an extravagant

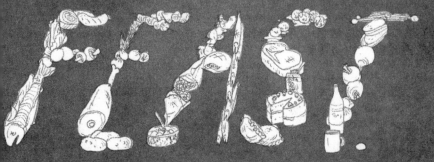

And the next day, her mother showed me how to make soap by mixing the ashes from their campfire with the fat of a Kemerovo pig."

49

Suddenly, Veronica has my full attention. This is *exactly* the sort of thing that Annabelle might have done. In fact, it's precisely the sort of thing that Annabelle *has* done! In

Volume 34: **Tastes Like Chicken,**

she saves the High Priestess of Yrgenblight's daughter from certain peril and is rewarded with a feast of deep-fried

WORM WAFFLES!

In Annabelle's case, instead of a wolf pack, the little girl was cornered by a **LASER-EYED** cyborg hyena invented by Annabelle's nemesis, Dr. Fungo.

I am suddenly full of questions.

How did you scare off the wolves?

By yelling loudly and waving my arms aggressively and maintaining constant eye contact. I had to make them think I was a threat.

Weren't you scared?

She didn't have *time* to be scared. It was pure INSTINCT,

says Hilly, who seems to have heard the story before.

Veronica smiles modestly. "It's what anyone would have done under those circumstances."

But it isn't, of course. Only someone quite *extraordinary* would—or even could—have done such a thing. Veronica has had adventures as thrilling as Annabelle's. But Annabelle is a character in a book, and Veronica is a *real-live person, right in front of me*! For the sake of my mission, I try not to seem excited. But between you and me, I ABSOLUTELY AM

Veronica turns to us
and holds her three middle
fingers in the air, and all of us hold
ours up in reply. "Thank you, Scouts.
That's it for tonight. Please remember
to bring me your permission slips for next
Friday's camping trip."

I don't camp, of course. For no other reason
than spiders, which have two more legs than I
am entirely comfortable with. But I, Moxie
McCoy, am committed to this case. If Wonder
Scouts camp, then I camp, because *I am a
Wonder Scout*. Or so it must seem.

Deep inside my soul, I wince for
being so thoroughly devoted to
my work.

After the meeting, I go up
to the girl with the sassy glasses.

Thanks for nominating me.

No problem, she says, holding
out her hand.

I'm Hilly.

She has a surprisingly firm grip, like she actually means it.

"Why haven't I met you before?"

"I'm homeschooled."

"*Home*schooled?"

"My parents give me a STACK of BOOKS to READ.
We talk about them. We go to museums and national parks
and artists' studios. It's pretty great."

How I wish I could go to school at home! But
Dad is gone all day at the bicycle factory. And even
when Mom's not in the submarine, she is often
elsewhere in the world, studying insects for the
good of humanity. Plus, being at home would make
it much harder to acquire new cases, since there has
never been much calamity in Casa McCoy.

"What's *her* story?" I ask, gesturing to Veronica, who seems, at this moment, to be demonstrating proper push-up technique to . . . what's her name? . . . Henrietta Bork.

I'm struggling to figure out how someone as amazing as Veronica could be in charge of such an awful organization as Wonder Scouts.

"These days, she's a librarian here in town," says Hilly.

I suddenly realize where I've seen Veronica before—restocking shelves in my third-favorite building, the Tiddlywhump Public Library!

"But before that, she traveled the world." Hilly gets a look of dreamy admiration. "That story she told tonight is just the TIP OF THE ICEBERG. Wait until you hear the rest."

"Can't wait," I say. I do not mention that I will use what I hear to end the so-called wonder.

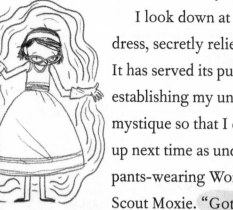

"So you know, we're not very fancy," says Hilly, smiling.

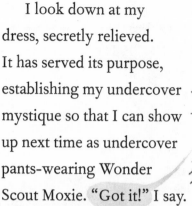

I look down at my dress, secretly relieved. It has served its purpose, establishing my undercover mystique so that I can show up next time as undercover pants-wearing Wonder Scout Moxie. "Got it!" I say.

"See you on Friday?" Hilly asks. She is making it difficult to dislike her, but I assume, since she is a Wonder Scout, that I just haven't figured out yet what makes her so awful.

"You certainly will."

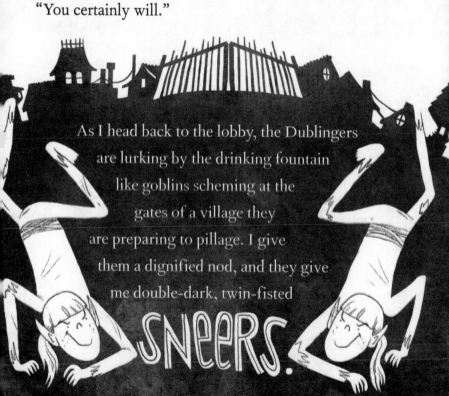

As I head back to the lobby, the Dublingers are lurking by the drinking fountain like goblins scheming at the gates of a village they are preparing to pillage. I give them a dignified nod, and they give me double-dark, twin-fisted SNEERS.

Dad is waiting when I get outside.

Well?

He has on his hopeful face.

It was great,

I say as I buckle my seat belt, because
I am technically undercover
until we're out of the parking lot.

When do you go back?

Friday. We meet three times a week.

Dad smiles. He and Mom have been trying to get me to
do an activity for the longest time.

When we get home, I tell Milton the truth.

There was nothing
wonderful about it.

What kind of accent
do they use?

Clearly, Milton has been
desperately wondering.

Tiddlewhumpian Schoolgirl.

Fascinating. Did you gather any clues?

56

"Not yet. The next badge challenge is on Friday. But Tracy spent 100% of the meeting looking 200% guilty."

"Don't jump to conclusions," says Milton. "We don't know for sure that someone is sabotaging Tammy's meringue. And if someone is, it isn't *necessarily* Tracy."

But it's just the sort of diabolical thing Tracy would do.

Which is why it seems a little too obvious, says Milton.

It could be *anyone.*

It could be Henrietta.

"Who?" I ask, but then I remember the sleepy robot who can't do push-ups. It seems impossible, but as much as I hate to admit it, Milton is usually not wrong.

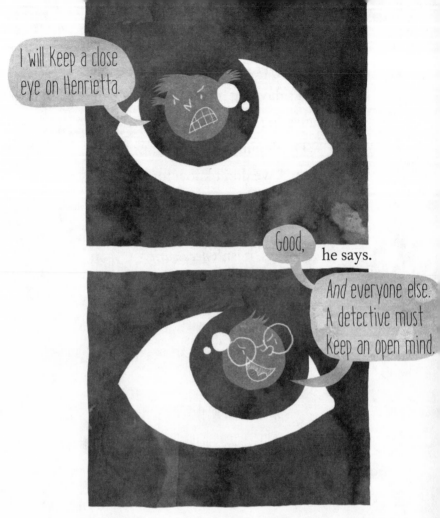

As much as dads like it when you repeat their wise thoughts, big sisters hate it when little brothers do the same thing. I am about to remind Milton that I am three years older and wiser, when he points to the which I have pinned to my sash with a safety pin.

"What's that?"

"Nothing," I say.
"Just part of my disguise."
I take off the sash as if it were ON FIRE
so Milton can see just how little I like it.

Before bed, I take a shower, eager to wash
the Wonder out of my hair. It takes a really
long time.

I stay up late reading the *Wonder
Scout Guidebook* and learn that two-
thirds of human beings have never
seen snow, that it is physically
impossible to lick your elbow, and that
a blue whale's fart bubble
is bigger than a
horse.

I glance at the list of 20 badges. It reminds me of everything I have not yet accomplished in life.

ARBORIST
Collect and identify leaf samples from 30 different kinds of trees.

ARTIST
Create and share something new and beautiful.

DETECTIVE
Use observation and deduction to solve a mystery.

EPIC BELCH
Achieve the ideal combination of volume, duration, and conviction.

INTREPID
Demonstrate genuine courage.

IRON GUT
Eat something highly unusual.

FIRE STARTER
Create a flame in less than two minutes without using matches.

FRIENDSMANSHIP
Perform an act of true friendship.

HISTORIAN
Discover and document an untold story of Tiddlywhump's past.

LOUDEST YELL
Shout loud enough to ring the Wonder Bell.

MASTER BAKER
Mix up a perfect
meringue in less
than five minutes.

MIGHTY
Demonstrate
extraordinary strength
(remember that there
are various kinds).

OBSCURE FACTS
Teach Veronica
something she
doesn't already know.

ORIENTEER
Find a hidden cache
using only your
map and compass.

PIG LATIN
Prove your fluency
by solving a riddle
told in pig Latin.

POLYGLOT
Count to ten
in seven
languages.

SCIENTIST
Use the scientific
method to explain
a natural
phenomenon.

SCRIBE
Write about an
experience that
made you change
your mind about
something.

STARING CONTEST
To claim the
badge, defeat the
current champion.

WONDER
Promise to keep
the secrets of
the Wonder Scouts.

I decide that as pointless as these badges might be, I should probably earn a few if I'm going to maintain my cover. Which won't be a problem. If Annabelle were a Wonder Scout, she would earn all 20 badges in about two weeks. And I am a lot like Annabelle.

I can belch like a TORNado,

I can yell like an AVALANCHE

and I create something *Beautiful,* every time I open my mouth.

I know many TRIVIAL FACTS,

I am strong like the delicious smell of  KIMCHI,

and I have earned the detective badge about

100 TIMES

already.

Have I ever met a challenge I can't meet? The answer is no, of course. Or maybe even **NO WAY.**

I look at the clock. It's technically way past time for bed, but I'm pretty sure I can learn to count to ten in seven languages before I go to sleep.

ICHI, NI, SAN...

CHAPTER 4: HOW MANY LEGS DOES A CENTIPEDE HAVE?

Thursday morning. Breakfast. I am reading the *Wonder Scout Guidebook*, and Milton is reading  again.

UNACCEPTABLE!

Apparently, I am supposed to care what's happening inside his head.

OUTRAGEOUS!

I consider responding but am far too busy learning how to pronounce the number seven in Hindi.

Multani is dropping the case!

says Milton, who is pacing back and forth like an ant whose hill just got smashed by a careless foot.

They're saying it was a "false alarm" and that there is "insufficient evidence to continue the investigation."

Isn't that a good thing?

Only if it's true,

he says.

Something doesn't quite add up. What about the **LOUD CRASH** in the basement?

I see why you're suspicious, but if Multani has closed the case, there must be a perfectly rational explanation.

But Milton is not convinced. "Something  is going on!"

I am entirely too busy with our *actual* case to devote any extra brain bits to second-guessing Multani. But this does seem like a perfect opportunity for Milton to work on his solo detective skills.

"Maybe you're right," I say. "Why don't you investigate?

The LOCAL HOUSE of HISTORY is only a few blocks from school. You could stop by on the way home."

Milton's eyes light up.

Will you come with me?

I like to reserve Thursday afternoons for reading Annabelle, but I could make an exception for the sake of helping my little brother get some practice on a case that has already been solved. "That *would* be rather nice of me, wouldn't it?"

Milton smiles like a puppy that has finally built up the courage to pounce on an unsuspecting DOG TREAT.

When we get to school, I see our fearless leader,

PRINCIPAL JONES,

who somehow seems taller and nobler and wiser than she did even yesterday.

I wonder if she has ever stared down a pack of wolves. I have no doubt she could and would if someone needed rescuing.

I give her a dignified nod, and she gives me a dignified nod, and we both agree without saying a word that Tiddlywhump Elementary would be nothing without us.

"Good morning, Moxie."

"Good morning, Principal Jones."

"You have the look of someone who is working on a new case." Principal Jones is very

OBSERVANT.

It's one of the things I like best about her.

I lean in close to keep our conversation confidential. "Indeed I am. A case of such consequence that it might well determine the future of the great town of Tiddlywhump . . . and beyond."

"Is that so?" asks Principal Jones, raising her beautiful right eyebrow in a way that makes me extremely jealous.

"Oh yes, it's so," I say, and then to make sure she truly understands, "It's *so* . . . so."

In that case, I thank you on behalf of Tiddlywhump . . . and beyond. Good luck, Moxie.

Most of the time, I would tell you that solving cases is a matter of skill, not luck, but if the luck in question is coming from Principal Jones, you can bet I'm going to take it.

By keeping my *Wonder Scout Guidebook* hidden inside my binder and reading it carefully while pretending to take notes, I am able to learn that centipedes don't *actually* have 100 legs with the *left* side of my brain while learning the basics of orienteering with the *right* side. It might be the first time that my

GREAT BIG HUNGRY MIND

has been adequately fed while sitting in a fourth-grade classroom.

"And how many legs does a centipede *actually* have, Moxie?" asks Mr. Shine.

"Way more than it should!" I say, and the class laughs, and so does Mr. Shine, because he is the sort of person who can appreciate a *good* answer as much as the *right* one.

The bell RINGS again, and it's time for recess.

69

"Could you stay behind for a minute, Moxie?"

I have a feeling I'm about to get scolded, which I probably deserve, but I do appreciate that Mr. Shine is the kind of teacher who yells at you in private.

"It seemed like you might not have been paying full attention this morning."

I think about making up some elaborate excuse for

WHY I COULD NOT CONCENTRATE,

but then I conclude that Mr. Shine will probably find the truth even more persuasive.

The truth is, I *have* been paying attention to the lesson, but I've *also* been busy learning other things at the same time.

Oh? What sorts of things?

"I have just joined the Wonder Scouts and have some catching up to do," I say, showing Mr. Shine my guidebook. "At the moment, I'm learning to count to ten in the world's seven most commonly spoken languages."

  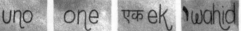

"I thought you weren't a fan of the Wonder Scouts."

I didn't realize that my opinion of the Wonder Scouts was so widely known.

"I'm *not*, of course. It's a shoddy organization full of badge-obsessed ninnies in ridiculous costumes."

"Then, why are you—?"

"Can I tell you something . . . *privately*?"

"Of course."

I lower my chin and look up at Mr. Shine with the utmost seriousness, just as Annabelle does when reporting top secret details to living legend and Girl Detective mission chief, Em.

"I'm only in Wonder Scouts as part of an . . .

Mr. Shine's eyes grow appropriately wide. "I see."

"Which means I can't give you the details, I'm afraid."

"Of course."

"Also, even though the Wonder Scouts themselves are an unsavory lot, their leader is not so bad. Her name is Veronica, and she is rather *INSPIRING*

"Inspiring?"

"I do not use the term lightly."

"I imagine you wouldn't. Now . . . believe it or not," says Mr. Shine, changing gears, "when I was your age, my friend Ronnie and I used to get a kick out of learning the basics of various languages, so I'm somewhat familiar with a few of the ones on your list."

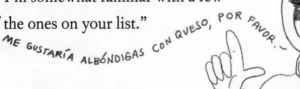

Knowing Mr. Shine, I am not surprised in the least. In addition to being one of the kindest people I know, he's also an extremely smart guy. And I'm guessing his friend Ronnie was, too.

"So . . . how about we spend recess practicing your Arabic and Hindi, and you agree to learn fourth-grade stuff between recess and lunch?"

"That sounds like a marvelous plan."

Mr. Shine smiles.

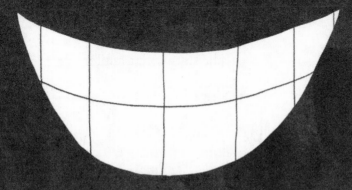

It's what he does best.

CHAPTER 5: A DIFFERENT KIND OF MYSTERY

The final bell rings. I am standing in front of the school, waiting for Milton, when I see Wonder Scout Hilly looking around for something or someone.

I'm about to say *Hello, Hilly!* when I remember I can't let her see me without my disguise. I slip on my glasses and sash and do my best to situate Emily's headband so that I will look like the gleaming tower of wonder Hilly expects me to be.

Hello, Hilly, I say.

What are you doing here?

Looking for you, she says with a smile.

I'm headed to Tiddlywhump Commons to identify trees for my Arborist badge. Want to come?

She holds up a book called

Field Guide to TREES.

I have the vague sense that there's something *else* I'm supposed to be doing, but I can't pass up the opportunity to get more insider information about the Wonder Scouts.

Plus, looking down at my own naked blue sash next to Hilly's cornucopia of colorful embroidery, I realize I have some catching up to do.

As we walk toward the Commons, I notice that Hilly is chewing gum. I am not allowed to have gum. Despite the fact that Mom and Dad are the two greatest parents in the history of Earth and every other planet, they have a terrible attitude about gum.

"Can I please have some gum?"

"Sure."

Hilly has the

FANCY KIND OF GUM

that comes in a long rectangular strip and is wrapped in actual tinfoil. I suddenly have the sense that she and I are going to get along fine.

Even though I've lived in Tiddlywhump my entire life and have been to the Commons at least 10,000 times, I've never paid much attention to the trees, which are, according to Hilly, an official arboretum planted many years ago by beloved Tiddlywhump philanthropist and arts patroness Julia Wonder.

I'm trying to decide whether there is anything more boring than trees when Hilly picks up a leaf and hands it to me.

"Our mission is to figure out what kind of tree it's from. What do you think *this* is, for example?" Hilly beams up at a tree as if it were the Statue of Liberty.

I look at the tree. It's a *tree*.

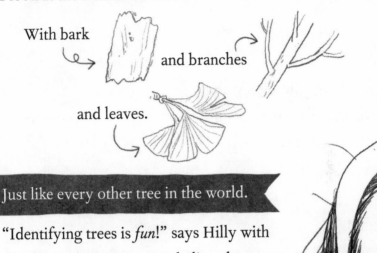

With bark and branches and leaves.

Just like every other tree in the world.

"Identifying trees is *fun*!" says Hilly with a smile that makes me want to believe her. "It's kind of like solving a *mystery*."

My ears perk up at the sound of my favorite word. "How so?"

"Look," she says.

"The leaf is full of clues.

This book is full of information.

Put them together and you have the solution."

I'm not quite convinced.

"Okay, what's this?" she
asks, holding up the leaf.

I wonder if it's a trick question. "A leaf?"

"Great!" she says. "You've just
eliminated all the trees in the conifer family,
which have needles instead of leaves.
Next . . . does the leaf have lobes?"

"What do you mean?"

"Red
maple leaves have
from three to
five lobes.

"Red oak
leaves have
from seven
to eleven."

NOPE.

"How many lobes does this one have?"
"Uh . . . zero?"
"Exactly! That's another *huge* clue."

Hilly flips through the pages of her book. We go through
a series of questions. The answer to each one narrows the
list of options.

"Let's see . . . is it shaped like a fan?"

"Yes."

"Then it must be a . . ." Hilly hands me the book, which has a picture of a leaf that looks exactly like the one in my hand.

"Ginkgo?"

"Exactly!" she says, laughing and handing me a plastic bag. "Put your leaf in this bag and write a little note with the name."

I do it.

It is kind of like sliding the critical clue into an EVIDENCE BAG.

"Great!" she says. "Only twenty-nine more to go!"

I think about groaning, but Hilly is having such a good time that I don't want to rain on her LEMONADE stand.

For the next few hours, Hilly and I walk around collecting leaves and using her book to figure out what kinds of trees they are from. We have just identified the leaf of an **EASTERN COTTONWOOD** that looks just like the spade in a deck of cards, when I notice how not-very-light the sky has become.

Hilly notices, too. "I'd better head home."

I look at my watch. It's **8:15**, and I'm almost late for dinner. "Me too!" I say. "But thanks!"

Seventeen trees! says Hilly, looking at her notebook.

We're more than halfway there.

Good night!

Hilly marches off. She must live on this side of the Commons.

To get home, I'll have to go through the middle of the park, which is growing darker by the minute. If I am to be entirely honest, I do not like the dark, and when I say I do not like it, I mean I like it less than mermaids like riding camels.

I think of a line from the Wonder Scout Credo—

The shortest route is not always best.

It suddenly sounds like excellent advice. It takes twice as long, but instead of cutting through the woods, I walk all the way around the Commons, sticking to the sidewalks and streetlamps. Perhaps it's unlikely that something shiny and purple with 17 bloody fangs and not quite 100 skittering legs will creep from the forest and drag me back to its damp and smelly lair, but I'd prefer not to take any chances.

When I get home and explain to Dad where I've been, he says, "No problem." He is chopping potatoes and swaying his hips while humming a heavy-metal rock song.

But Milton is piping mad. It's clear he wants to tell me all about it, but not in front of Dad.

Did you know that ginkgo trees have been around for 350 million years?

I ask.

I did not, says Dad.

Tell me more.

And so I tell him about the unusual shape of the ginkgo leaf and how the fruit smells like rotting butter as it ripens.

Throughout dinner, Milton simmers like a teakettle that's about to boil. As soon as we clear our plates and Dad goes out to the garage to tinker with his motorcycle, Milton starts spouting his flavorful opinions all over the living room.

I blink at Milton
like a bored old frog
blinks at nothing at all.

"You were supposed to come with me to
the Local House of History!"

"I wasn't *definitely* going to come."

"You were definitely going to come!"

Milton is starting to turn purple, and I worry that
his eyeballs might actually pop out, so I decide to
calm him down by saying "sorry," which is a thing I
try to do as seldom as possible.

"I'm sorry. I was working on the Wonder Scouts case.
Did you go by yourself?"

Milton turns from mad to sheepish,
which is much less awful to look at.

"Yes, but it didn't go well."

"What happened?"

"Chief Historian Bernard Buxton."

"Who's that?" I ask, but then I remember. "Beady eyes, crooked neck, nose like the beak of a falcon?"

"Exactly!" says Milton, shuddering a little.

Chief Historian Bernard Buxton is the thoroughly unpleasant person who led my class field trip, showing us this and that, forbidding us to touch anything, and failing to sufficiently acknowledge the greatness of Columbus.

"What happened?"

"Well, at first I couldn't find him."

"He wasn't at his desk? You could have run off with a priceless artifact!"

"I never would!" Milton is scandalized at the suggestion.

"What happened when he finally appeared?"

"He came up from the basement carrying a box. But before he even set it down, he locked the basement door behind him. It was *highly suspicious*!"

I consider telling Milton that carrying boxes and locking doors hardly qualifies as criminal activity, but he seems so excited that I don't have the heart. "What happened next?"

"I asked him about the break-in, but he told me, and I quote,

This, of course, is unacceptable. If the Chief Historian will not talk to children, how can they become informed citizens? How are they supposed to with civic pride?

I am tempted to march down to the Local House of History at this very moment, but I do not, because (1) it is bedtime, and (2) the Chief Historian is probably at home practicing his scowling, and (3) this is the perfect opportunity to coach Milton on his interrogation skills.

You need to march back down there tomorrow and let him know who's boss.

Milton is confused.

Isn't *he* the boss?

NO, Milton! *You* are the boss!

I am?

It's like helping a newborn lamb take its first, wobbly steps.

You *are*!

But he is the chief.

Chief of what?

Milton pauses, considering this.

History?

"Okay, so maybe he's the Chief Historian. But you, Milton McCoy, are the Chief . . .

Mysterian."

Milton's eyes get wide. He likes this. He likes it a lot.

"Yes," he says, standing proud and lifting his chin, "I am."

As he walks back down the hallway to his bedroom, I hear him repeating, "Milton McCoy, Chief Mysterian, at your service," under his breath.

I look in my mirror and give myself a double thumbs-up. I have done my work for the day. I have earned my rest.

CHAPTER 6: MOXIE'S MENTAL HEALTH DAY

The morning comes. I can't possibly go to school today. I have far too much to learn. I must prepare for tonight's Wonder Scout meeting and cannot be bothered with

spelling

rose rows roes

and pronouns

I you her she

and raising my hand whenever I have a question.

I lie in bed and moan until Dad comes to ask me what's wrong. I tell him I might be dying, and he gives me a thermometer. When he goes down the hall to brush his teeth, I warm it against the lightbulb of my reading lamp.

Dad comes back.

It looks like you have a temperature of a hundred and fifty-seven.

That sounds worrisome.

"It's terrible," he says. "We should get you to the hospital *immediately*. Unless . . . there's some chance that this thermometer is malfunctioning?"

"That's probably it," I say, eager to change the subject.

"You're *not* dying?"

"Probably not, but I stayed up all night reading Annabelle, and I'm extremely fatigued." I figure *fatigued* sounds much more serious than just plain *tired*.

I pretend to suddenly fall asleep and make a few extremely convincing snores. I open my eyes to see if the coast is clear, but Dad is still standing there.

"Are you suddenly feeling better?" he asks.

"I've been giving it some serious thought . . ." I say, which is how Dad starts sentences when trying to convince Mom that she should definitely agree with whatever he's going to say next.

"The next Wonder Scout badge challenge is tonight, and there are *so many things* I need to learn! There are so many *other things* I need to practice! If I were to attend tonight's meeting in this state of crippling ignorance, I might bring shame upon our family name!" I stand up on my bed to emphasize the impending calamity.

"That sounds serious," says Dad.

I remember to lie down again.

I would probably recover from my sudden unexpected illness much more quickly if I were to spend all day in bed reading my *Wonder Scout Guidebook*.

Is that so?

Oh, definitely. And furthermore, I am entirely certain that Mom would agree.

Dad is considering.

So, you would be spending the day reading?

Yes.

And learning?

Absolutely.

And not watching television?

Of course not!

I am shocked that Dad would consider such a thing.

"All right, then. How about we call it . . . a *mental health day*?"

"What's that?"

"Every once in a long, long, *long* while, I think it's okay to take a day off from school just because you need to."

Suddenly, I love my dad even more than I did five minutes ago, which causes my heart to expand unexpectedly, which hurts a little but is entirely necessary in order to keep love from leaking out of my heart and onto my shirt.

"Yes, that sounds like *exactly* what I need."

"I can drive you to school today, friend," says Dad to Milton, who is standing in the doorway, rolling his eyes and shaking his head at the very same time.

I give Milton a smile and a wink as he frowns his way out the door. And I am left with an empty house and GREAT, ENDLESS HEAPS of MENTAL HEALTH.

I consider starting my beautiful day by demonstrating my **LOUDEST** yell. but worry I might frighten the neighbors, so instead I practice the related body motions, which involve

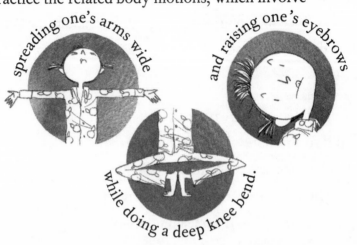

spreading one's arms wide

and raising one's eyebrows

while doing a deep knee bend.

I glance down the list of badges.

Do I need to practice lifting heavy objects?

I scoff at the notion.

Can I start a fire without matches?

Does a leaping lemur leap?

I think about looking up some obscure fact,

but my brain is an encyclopedia of fascinating details.

And I could win a staring contest

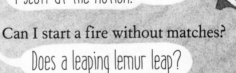

with my eyes closed.

I decide that my  **VAST OCEANS OF NATURAL TALENT** have left me thoroughly prepared, that there is nothing left to practice, and that my day of mental health belongs to Annabelle.

I start with Volume 18: *Born That Way,* in which Annabelle is thrust into a series of utterly unfamiliar situations (piloting a damaged helicopter, taming an irritated cobra, and defusing a ticking time bomb) but miraculously masters them all with "grace and aplomb" (which I figure is something like a plum).

I read and I read and I read.

Moxie!

I have the sense that an eager gnome is examining my shoulder.

Wake up,

says Milton, who seems to think he's waking me up, which is impossible because I do not and never nap.

It's time for dinner.

I am about to laugh at the hilarious joke, when I notice it's getting dark outside. I look at the clock, and it's absolutely true. I have definitely been not taking a nap for a very long time.

Which means we need to eat dinner quickly so that we can get to Wonder Scouts on time! Which means there is no time to practice counting to ten in seven languages, which doesn't matter because my mind is an

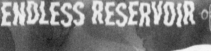

ENDLESS RESERVOIR of KNOWLEDGE.

After dinner, Dad drives me to the community center. The meeting begins. We sing the song of Wonder. We recite the Credo. Then Veronica speaks.

Raise your hand if you would like to challenge for a badge.

Tammy raises her hand. Tracy raises her hand. Henrietta looks as if she'd really like to raise her hand but can't because it weighs a thousand pounds.

Chin up, Henrietta, says Veronica.

Henrietta raises her head.

Eyes up.

Henrietta raises her eyes to look at Veronica for just a moment, then lowers them again. Veronica doesn't press the point.

A young woman should hold her head high, says Veronica.

She should make eye contact whenever she speaks. Each of you must strive to find your voice. Because each of you has something important to add to the world.

Henrietta, I have the sense that you'd like to challenge for a badge this evening. Is that correct?

Ever so hesitantly, Henrietta nods.

Voice, please.

Uh . . . yes.

Excellent. Anyone else?

Before I know it, I raise my right hand, and then my left one, too, suddenly convinced that just one hand is not enough to adequately communicate my level of interest in challenging for a badge. "Very well," says Veronica. "Who would like to go first?"

"I would," say Tammy and Henrietta at the exact same time.

Tammy plows through her like a bulldozer obliterating a pile of mini marshmallows.

I'd like to challenge for the Master Baker badge.

"I thought you might," says Veronica with a twinkle in her eye. "Which means we might all get to witness the moment when the first Scout earns her **20ᵀᴴ** badge!"

There is a murmur of excitement from all but one of the Scouts.

"*I'll* get the supplies," says Tracy, in a way that is meant to *sound* helpful but is completely unconvincing.

"I'd rather you *didn't*," says Tammy, in a way that is meant to suggest she trusts Tracy about as far as she can throw a piano.

"Now, *Tammy*," says Veronica, "a Wonder Scout must always depend on the kindness of her fellow Scouts. *You* take a moment to focus and prepare. Let Tracy get the supplies."

While Tammy takes a moment to glower and fume,
Tracy goes into the kitchen and comes back with the mixer, a
bowl, and various ingredients.

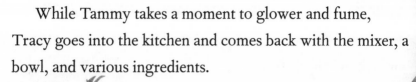

"Here you go, *sister*," says Tracy,
as if she were a knitting needle and
Tammy a helpless balloon.

"Thank you, *sister*," says
Tammy, as if she were a machete
and Tracy a cluster of thistles.

With the mechanical precision of a robot ninja warrior,
Tammy cracks six eggs,

separates out the yolks,

adds some

CREAM
of
TARTAR

and turns on
the mixer.

Egg whites beaten with such fury should
promptly rise into the most magnificent
meringue the world has ever seen, and yet . . .
the eggs do not stiffen, and we let out a collective
SIGH of DISMAY.

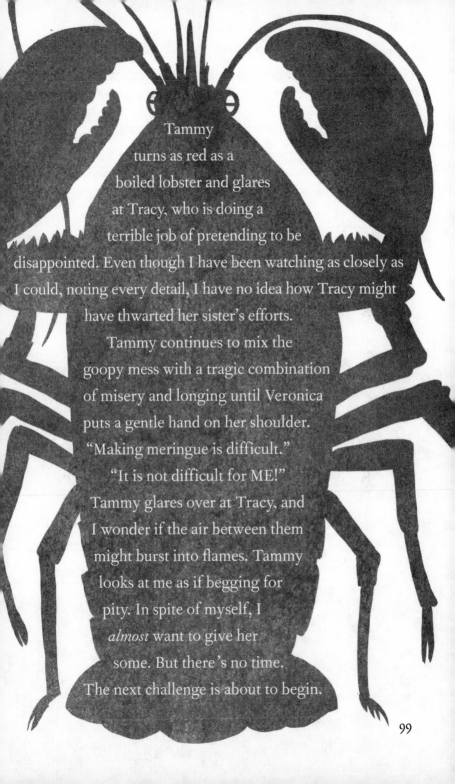

Tammy
turns as red as a
boiled lobster and glares
at Tracy, who is doing a
terrible job of pretending to be
disappointed. Even though I have been watching as closely as
I could, noting every detail, I have no idea how Tracy might
have thwarted her sister's efforts.

Tammy continues to mix the
goopy mess with a tragic combination
of misery and longing until Veronica
puts a gentle hand on her shoulder.
"Making meringue is difficult."
"It is not difficult for ME!"
Tammy glares over at Tracy, and
I wonder if the air between them
might burst into flames. Tammy
looks at me as if begging for
pity. In spite of myself, I
almost want to give her
some. But there's no time.
The next challenge is about to begin.

"Who would like to go next?" asks Veronica.

"*I'll* go," say Tracy and Henrietta at the exact same time. Once again, Henrietta gets flattened. Like a daisy in a garden where a Dublinger is dancing.

"I'll challenge for Orienteering," says Tracy. Now it's Tammy's turn to look worried as Tracy takes out her map and compass.

Veronica turns and looks out the window. "I don't know, Tracy. Orienteering is more of a daytime activity. It's AWFULLY DARK OUT THERE.

Tracy scoffs. "I have a flashlight. Plus, shouldn't a Scout be able to find her way in the dark?"

"I admire your mettle," says Veronica, handing Tracy a piece of paper. "Here are your coordinates." She turns to us with a smile. "Here is another opportunity for the first Scout to earn her twentieth badge!"

Tracy opens the back door and races into the darkness with a look of fiercest determination.

Where's she going?

I ask Hilly.

Veronica hid a cache somewhere in the soccer field behind the community center. Now Tracy has to find it using only her compass and map.

That sounds hard.

It is. But Tracy is really good at it. So it's weird that she's challenged for the badge three times and still hasn't found the cache.

would you describe it as... suspiciously weird?

I watch Hilly's face as my question runs through an obstacle course in her head.

Yeah. I guess I would.

Veronica speaks. "While Tracy is orienteering, let's have another challenge."

"I'll go!" I say.

"Very well, Moxie. Which badge are you going to challenge for?"

The list of badges is like a pile of presents, and I want to open them all. My mouth starts making words before my brain can remember what they actually mean.

All of them.

All of them?

All of them!

Tammy makes a face like a hailstorm.

YOU ONLY GET ONE BADGE CHALLENGE PER NIGHT!!

That is usually the case, Moxie,

says Veronica.

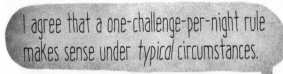

I agree that a one-challenge-per-night rule makes sense under *typical* circumstances.

Typical circumstances?

Typical circumstances. But since I'm going to be camping next weekend, I feel an obligation to prove my readiness for life on the savage frontier, *if only for the safety of my fellow* Scouts!

Veronica succeeds in swallowing her smile, but I can tell I've won her over. "All right, *for the safety of your fellow Scouts*, you may challenge for . . . three."

Tammy makes a face like summer vacation has just been

===(**CANCELED.**)===

"I think I can save us all some time by starting with the Detective badge. I have solved dozens of mysteries this year alone. Perhaps you have heard of my work on

I hold out my hand, waiting for my badge, imagining how nice it will look on my sash.

"I have not," says Veronica. "But if you're such a skilled detective, you should have no problem solving a *new* mystery. To earn the  you must *first* describe the mystery you're trying to solve to your fellow Scouts and *then* share the solution. Do you have a mystery in mind?"

I want to tell Veronica that asking me to solve a new mystery is like asking a world-famous brain surgeon to put a bandage on a toddler's elbow, but it's clear there's no changing her mind.

"I'll think of one for the next meeting," I say. "For now, I will challenge for the Mighty badge instead."

"Very well," says Veronica. "How are you going to demonstrate your EXTRAORDINARY STRENGTH?"

I look around for some barbells or a boulder, but the heaviest thing in the room seems to be a potted plant in the corner. Using proper technique (bent knees, straight back—thank you, Dad!), I lift it *effortlessly*! Except that it is much heavier than it looks. I do not lift it a lot. But I do get it sort of halfway off the ground.

I give a satisfied SIGH the way superheroes do when they have conquered one or more of life's great challenges.

"Nice try," says Veronica, "but that's not the type of strength we're looking for. This badge recognizes strength of *character*."

I am **OUTRAGED!** If lifting massive objects is not allowed, the guidebook should be clearer!

"In that case, I would like to challenge for the OBSCURE FACTS BADGE."

"All right," says Veronica. "Tell me something I don't know."

I thumb through my inner dictionary of fantastic facts. It's like picking apples in an endless orchard.

Hummingbirds weigh less than a penny.

"That is a wonderful, interesting fact, but . . . I already knew it."

I am discouraged but by no means defeated. I reach into even deeper corners of my vast and powerful brain.

Cotton candy was invented by a dentist.

"Another fascinating piece of information . . . that I have previously encountered."

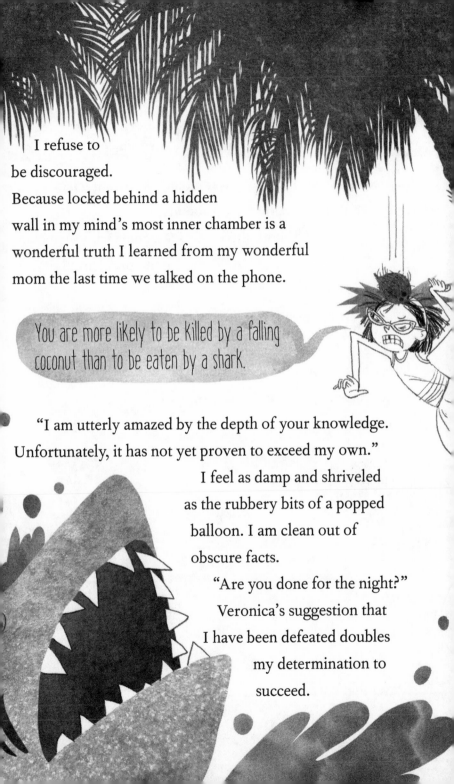

I refuse to
be discouraged.
Because locked behind a hidden
wall in my mind's most inner chamber is a
wonderful truth I learned from my wonderful
mom the last time we talked on the phone.

You are more likely to be killed by a falling
coconut than to be eaten by a shark.

"I am utterly amazed by the depth of your knowledge.
Unfortunately, it has not yet proven to exceed my own."

I feel as damp and shriveled
as the rubbery bits of a popped
balloon. I am clean out of
obscure facts.

"Are you done for the night?"
Veronica's suggestion that
I have been defeated doubles
my determination to
succeed.

"I'm just getting started! How about the Polyglot badge?"

"That's a tough one," says Veronica. "Are you sure you're ready?"

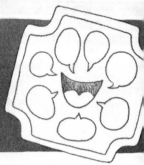

"Sure as Sherman," I say, not really knowing what it means, but really liking how it sounds.

"All right, then," says Veronica with a chuckle. I count to ten in Spanish, no problem. I've known Spanish since I was two.

Russian is a little bumpy, but I manage to bumble through. But then I get to Mandarin Chinese, and my brain gets murky. It's almost impossible to concentrate with twelve sets of eyes staring at you.

And that's where my locomotive mind runs out of steam.

So I try Annabelle's proven technique for abruptly changing topics when she finds herself at a dead end. I jump up suddenly and wave my hands excitedly and point enthusiastically to the other side of the room so that everyone will wonder what's going on over there and won't remember what I was talking about before.

It works! Everyone is extremely confused. "What I *meant* to say is that I wanted to challenge for . . . Loudest Yell."

"All . . . right . . ." says Veronica, who is probably not fooled but seems perhaps to appreciate my persistence. "Now remember, you must yell loudly enough to make the Wonder Bell ring." She points to a copper bell hanging at the far side of the room.

No problem, I say.

I happen to be the loudest human being I've ever met.

At the count of three, says Veronica.

One, two, three . . .

I YELL SO LOUDLY

that people cringe in Indonesia.
Or so I assume. My yell ends, and I wait for the pleasant
sound of the Wonder Bell ringing. But all I hear is the
lonesome sound of NOTHING AT ALL.

The bell must be broken! I insist.

It rang just fine last week, says Tammy.

It's *impossible* that it wouldn't have rung, I protest.

I'm *that* loud.

Atwhay away oserlay!

says Tammy Dublinger under her breath.

I have no idea what she's talking about, but Hilly
scowls as if Tammy has said something truly awful.

"I'd like to challenge for the . . ." I scan the list for some sign of hope.

"I think you've had enough chances for tonight," says Veronica. "Perhaps you could stand to *practice* a bit."

I am fuming at the suggestion that I need to practice. I *did* practice! For at least *20 minutes*!

Just then, Tracy Dublinger returns, looking like a

FIRECRACKER

with a very short fuse.

"It seems you didn't find the cache," says Veronica kindly. But Tracy is in no mood to be consoled.

"There's something wrong with my compass!"

"Let's see," says Veronica. She lifts up a chain that's hanging around her neck. Attached is a

COMPASS

that gleams golden like the sun.

"Tell us the story of how you got your compass!" says Hilly.

"Not now," says Veronica, holding her compass next to Tracy's.

  point in the same direction.

"Looks like your compass is working just fine," says Veronica. "Maybe you need to brush up on your map skills."

"My map skills are *excellent*!"

"I'm sure they are," says Veronica. "But perhaps they could be *even better*. Remember, Scouts," says Veronica, looking at all of us now, "if you know your weaknesses, you'll know how to work around them. If you know your strengths, you'll know how to use them to get what you want."

Veronica is an empress surrounded by loyal subjects. It's impossible not to feel a bit of awe.

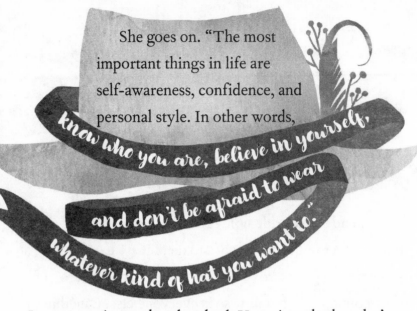

She goes on. "The most important things in life are self-awareness, confidence, and personal style. In other words, *know who you are, believe in yourself, and don't be afraid to wear whatever kind of hat you want to.*"

I want to raise my hand and ask Veronica whether she's talking about an actual hat, but I'm pretty sure she's not, so I don't.

"And remember, *always* remember . . ." Veronica pauses and looks out at us, waiting.

GIRLS CAN DO ANYTHING!

say all the Scouts together. Except for me. I believe that I can do anything, of course, but I am far too original to say it just because everyone else does.

I spend the car ride home rehashing the events of the past hour. Never in the history of Moxie McCoy have I failed at so many things in a row. Not only am I firmly aware of my shortcomings . . . but now so is everyone else. One thing I know is, they won't remain shortcomings for long. If I can wear any hat I choose, I'll wear one that's covered with Wonder Scout badges.

When I get home, I hug Dad good night and curl up in bed with my *Wonder Scout Guidebook*. But where my bookmark should be, there's a note.

Pig Latin is easy.
I'll teach you.
Tiddlywhump Commons,
8:00 a.m. tomorrow?

— Helly

First I call  to ask if she'll join me in the park in the morning. But she's already asleep, so I leave a message with one of her dads. I'm not sure which one.

And then I put on my fierce face and dig in to the

CHALLENGE·AT·HAND

practicing counting to ten in seven languages,

  studying various wilderness fire-starting techniques,

and trying to figure out how to demonstrate extraordinary strength without using my extraordinary muscles.

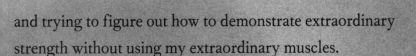

CHAPTER 7: OXIEMAY, ILLYHAY, AND EMILYWAY

My alarm rings at 5:45 a.m. I leave a note for Dad and head out for Tiddlywhump Commons. It's just getting light by the time I reach the edge of the woods. A few minutes later, Emily appears, loyal as a well-thrown boomerang, reliable as a solar-powered calculator on a sunny day.

Thank you for coming!

I say.

I do not say,

Thank you for coming so that I do not have to be alone in the creepy forest while I identify leaves for my Arborist badge.

No problem, she says.

I am all for enjoying the great outdoors.

So . . . why are we here at this . . . perfectly *reasonable* hour?

"I thought it might be fun to identify some trees. Also, my new friend Hilly from Wonder Scouts is coming a little later, and I want you to meet her. She seems okay, but since she is, as you know, a Wonder Scout, I would appreciate a *Second ✌ Opinion.*"

Emily smiles. "If you like her, I'm sure she's great."

As we walk through the woods looking for new trees, I wow Emily by counting to ten in Bengali.

"You seem to be enjoying Wonder Scouts."

"OH YES, WONDER SCOUTS IS THE BEST,"

I say as loudly as I can.

Then, as quietly as I can, so as not to be overheard in the likely case that my enemies have hidden surveillance microphones in the nearby bushes, I say,

I still have deep suspicions, but you were right that not all of them are horrible.

How wonderful!

says Emily as loudly as she can.
Under her breath she says,

What are you still suspicious about?

I love your unicorn brooch!

I say as loudly as I can.
Under my breath I say,

Well, not only is Tracy sabotaging Tammy, but also I'm pretty sure that Tammy is doing the same to Tracy.

No!

I'm afraid so. It's *delicious!*

And what are the *good* parts of Wonder Scouts?

Well, Hilly seems pretty great so far. She goes to school at home.

Lucky!

I know!

And our leader is amazing. She's like a real-life Annabelle Adams.

How so?

Knowing that Veronica is extremely modest and prefers to keep her tales of daring under wraps, I look around to make sure no one is listening before leaning in close and speaking to Emily in a dramatic whisper:

"Last night I learned that she once raised a tiger cub to be her companion, and when it grew up, it guided her through a tiger-infested jungle to a hidden temple, where she discovered the long-lost scepter of the seven-headed serpent goddess Hisstrula, which she donated to a museum because she is not only bold but also quite generous."

"Really?" says Emily, as if I just said

Which I understand, because
what I am saying is so extraordinary.

"Really!"

"Hmm," says Emily, who is
obviously jealous and suddenly
reconsidering whether she should
join Wonder Scouts after all.

"Are you *sure* you don't want to join?"

"I'm sure," says Emily. "The GAS is so uncomfortable."

"Right." I find myself
wondering if there might
be some sort of medicine
that Emily could take.

"But I *do* want to hear more about what you're
learning," she adds.

"I'm afraid I can't tell you anything else."

"Why not?"

"It's all CLASSIFIED."

"I thought your plan was to expose the Wonder Scouts' secrets."

"It is, but . . ." I find myself torn between

wanting to expose the Wonder Scouts'

SECRETS

and wanting to protect them with my dying breath.

. . . being undercover is so confusing.

I can only imagine, says Emily.

How about you help me identify some trees?

Sounds like a plan.

And this is just another reason I love Emily so much. Because she's game for anything, even walking through the woods and looking for leaves before the sun is fully awake.

When my second alarm goes off at 7:45 a.m., I put on the headband and rhinestone glasses and give Emily a serious look.

Remember that for today I am not the Moxie McCoy you've known and loved all these long weeks. I am

MOXIE McCOY, WONDER SCOUT.

"Got it," says Emily.

When Hilly arrives at 8:00 a.m., I show her the seven new leaves Emily and I have identified.

"Holy wow!" says Hilly.

"You taught me everything I know," I say. And then I introduce my best friend to my new friend, realizing as I do how much I hope they'll like each other.

I hear you go to school at home, says Emily.

It's pretty much the greatest, says Hilly.

Jealous, says Emily.

So far, so good, I think.

While we wander the Commons identifying leaves, Hilly teaches us how to speak pig Latin, which is way less complicated than I feared it would be.

Here's how it works:

You take the first consonant sound of any word, move it to the end, and then add *ay*.

So, for *Moxie* . . .

. . . you move the *M* to the end and then add *ay*, for *Oxiemay*.

Which, if I must say, has a magnificent ring to it.

And then for *Hilly* . . .

. . . you move the *H* to the end and add *ay*, for *Illyhay*.

Which is pretty great, too.

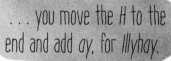

And for Emily . . .

. . . because it starts with a vowel sound, you just add *way*, for Emilyway.

Which is downright spectacular.

We spend a
long time practicing our
pig Latin, and then Hilly teaches us
how to navigate using a map and compass,
by picking spots in the park and telling us
the coordinates. As it turns out, finding
hidden treasures by orienteering is *also*
like solving a mystery.

It's technically against
the rules, but we sneak under
the Ample Creek bridge to eat lunch. Hilly
shares her orange soda, and we practice our belching.
"Why is belching a thing in Wonder Scouts?"
asks Emily.

"Veronica wants to make sure that each of us gets
a chance to see how good it can feel to be unladylike,"
says Hilly.

Emily lets out a fairly epic belch. "I see what she means."

When we're done eating, we tell one another all the obscure facts we can think of. Hilly is working on her Polyglot badge, too, so we drill each other back and forth, but she has trouble remembering the unfamiliar sounds of Mandarin Chinese, Hindi, and Arabic.

"My dad Jim always says it's way easier to remember things when you put them in a song," says Emily.

"What do you mean?" asks Hilly.

Peanut butter's sticky. And Mandarin is tricky!

I sing at the top of my lungs.

Hilly looks at me as if I've lost my mind, but I can tell she also kind of likes it.

But we have to learn it....

Emily sings, continuing the tune. But then she gets stuck looking for a matching rhyme.

Hilly's eyes flash with an idea.

There's a badge, I want to earn it,

she adds, and we collapse into a pile of giggles.

125

It takes a while, but we come up with a song that gets all the languages in.

"Does that help?" Emily asks.

"I think so," says Hilly. "I guess we'll find out."

Then we have a few staring contests, but neither Emily nor Hilly can come close to beating me, which makes sense, since neither is familiar with Annabelle's patented

DEEP ARCTIC STARE.

No matter how many times I try to show them how it works, they both start giggling the moment I pull it out.

"I'll never get that badge," says Hilly, laughing to herself. "And that's okay with me."

"Isn't the point to get every badge there is, and as soon as possible?" I ask.

"Nah. The point is to learn stuff and have fun. No one is good at everything."

I am about to tell her that *I* am, but I decide I don't need to actually *say* it, because I'm pretty sure Hilly already knows. Also, Veronica told us that the real point is

 instead of

And since I am pretending to be a Wonder Scout, I decide to pretend I don't need to brag about my endless talents.

Suddenly, it's almost dinnertime again.

"Iway adhay away eallyray icenay ayday," I say.

"Eemay ootay!" says Hilly.

"Icenay ootay eetmay ouyay, Illyhay," says Emily.

"Esyay itway asway!" says Hilly to Emily.

"Eesay ouyay Ondaymay?" says Hilly to me.

"Ouyay etbay!" I say.

As I walk back home, it occurs to me that at some point throughout the day, I might have forgotten about being undercover Wonder Scout Moxie and just started acting like Detective Super-Genius Moxie instead. I panic for a second, worrying that Hilly might have noticed.

 When I get home, I want to ask Milton what he thinks, but he is asleep on the couch. Dad says Milton spent the entire day reading the newspaper and yanking on his right earlobe, which is what he often does when trying to puzzle through a problem.

"Is something going on with him?" asks Dad.

"You know, he's just . . . Milton," I say, and Dad gives me a look that says, *Enough said. I know what you mean.*

The next morning, I open my bedroom door to find Milton waiting like a sinkhole in the middle of the sidewalk. And instead of saying Good morning. or How did you sleep? or Dearest sister, might I offer you some orange juice?

he gets right to the matter at hand.

"In yesterday morning's paper, there was an article about an upcoming exhibit at the Local House of History called

100 Years of Wonder

about beloved arts patron Julia Wonder and her legacy of generosity and service to the Town of Tiddlywhump."

"Is the exhibit somehow related to the alleged break-in?"

"It very well could be, but we won't know for sure until we interrogate the Chief Historian!"

"Can I assume you have not yet told him who's boss?"

Milton slumps. "I haven't."

Why not?

I just couldn't!

Why not?

He is extremely tall.

I shake my head. I want to explain to Milton that

 true height is nothing but a state of mind.

"But . . . you could come with me!" Milton's eyes are pleading. "*Together*, we could get him to talk!"

"I'm sorry, but I am extremely busy with the Case of the Thwarted Badge," I say, hoping to distract Milton into forgetting about the Local House of History. It seems to be working.

What progress have you made?

Well, I'm pretty sure that Tammy is sabotaging Tracy *and* that Tracy is sabotaging Tammy.

The old double double cross?

It seems likely.

Evidence?

I tell him about Tammy's amazing technique and how the meringue absolutely should have worked—and how Veronica checked Tracy's compass and found *nothing* wrong.

"It doesn't make any sense!" I insist.

Milton starts tugging on his ear. "I have a theory," he says with a sudden look of triumph.

This is exciting. "Let me hear it!"

NO!

he shouts, stomping his tiny right foot like a scrappy Chihuahua facing off against a massive rhinoceros.

I won't help you with your case until you help me with mine!

This is progress! Milton is trying to show *me* who's boss! Annabelle calls what Milton is demanding a QUID PRO QUO, which always makes me think of my favorite deep-fried appetizer but which is just another way of saying "I'll help you if you help me."

I'm all for helping Milton with his imaginary case if it means making progress with my real one.

"All right," I say. "Get your bike. Let's go to the Local House of History."

"Right now?"

"Right now."

On the one hand, I need to reward Milton for being such a tough guy.

On the other hand, I might be able to pick up some tidbits for my Historian badge.

And on the *third* hand, if I had one, I'm itching to let Chief Historian Bernard Buxton know who's *actually* boss.

"I'll be right back," says Milton. He then races to his room and reappears a moment later wearing a toddler-sized tool belt with every loop and pocket overflowing.

What . . . is *that?*

My gear.

Your gear?

Tweezers, duct tape, Swiss Army knife, nylon rope, sunblock, permanent marker, Magnetron 2000, water-purification tablets, antelope repellent.

Shall I go on?

I am equal parts jealous and proud. As I stand there at a loss for words, Milton finds some for me.

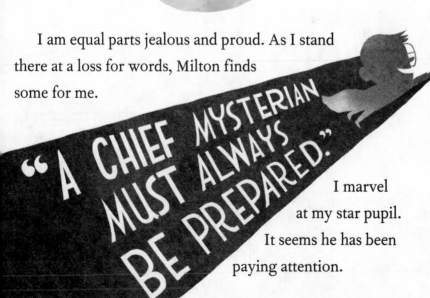

"A CHIEF MYSTERIAN MUST ALWAYS BE PREPARED."

I marvel at my star pupil. It seems he has been paying attention.

CHAPTER 8: CHIEF OF WHO, EXACTLY?

We tell Dad that we're heading to the Local House of History, which is true, but we don't tell him that we are heading there to tell Chief Historian Bernard Buxton who's actually boss. As Annabelle Adams often says, "Less is more, unless you're referring to pineapple upside-down cake."

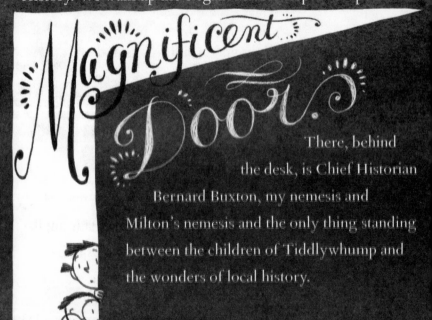

Have fun,

says Dad, grinning. He and Mom are always hoping I'll take more of an interest in Milton.

A few minutes later, we arrive at the Local House of History. We walk up the elegant marble steps and open the

Magnificent Door.

There, behind the desk, is Chief Historian Bernard Buxton, my nemesis and Milton's nemesis and the only thing standing between the children of Tiddlywhump and the wonders of local history.

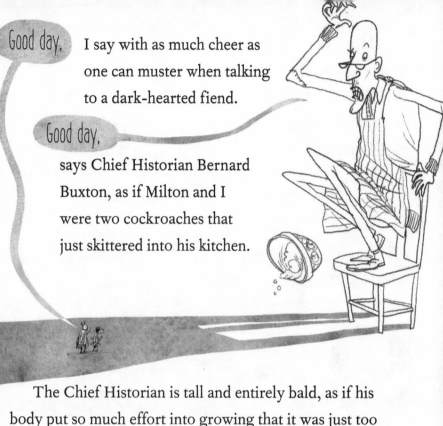

Good day, I say with as much cheer as one can muster when talking to a dark-hearted fiend.

Good day, says Chief Historian Bernard Buxton, as if Milton and I were two cockroaches that just skittered into his kitchen.

The Chief Historian is tall and entirely bald, as if his body put so much effort into growing that it was just too tired when it came time to make hair.

I launch into my interrogation, showing my little brother how it's done.

The name's Moxie. Moxie McCoy. I think you've met my fellow detective Milton. We're here to investigate the Case of the Invisible Intruder.

135

"I have no idea what you're talking about," says the Chief Historian as he busily starts dusting a glass case containing Marcus Tiddlywhump's favorite ∼ *hairbrush*

Let me refresh your memory:

a crash in the basement,

a call to the police,

a suspicious lack of clues.

"There was nothing *suspicious* about the lack of clues."

"You mean there was *nothing* out of the ordinary?"

"Nothing."

I glance over at Milton to make sure he is properly impressed with my performance, but instead of taking notes, he is looking around the room intently, as if trying to discover its deepest secrets.

 "So, there were no footprints or . . .

rusty weapons, or . . .

giant pools of blood?"

"Nothing at all. There wasn't even an intruder. Detective Multani concluded that there was insufficient evidence to continue the investigation."

While I give the Chief Historian a glimpse of Annabelle's patented Deep Arctic Stare with one eye, I use the other eye to notice that Milton is ever so slowly inching his way around the far side of COLUMBUS. I have no idea what he's up to, but the situation has just grown far more complicated.

Which is exactly how I like it.

If nothing happened, why did you call the police in the first place?

I had heard a crash in the basement.

My extra eye watches as Milton removes the

MAGNETRON 2000

from his tool belt and carefully extends the shaft, which grows LONGER and LONGER like an endlessly unfolding telescope. He gives me an urgent pleading look, and my mission is clear—keep the Chief Historian occupied.

Could you describe it for me?

Chief Historian
Bernard Buxton
sniffles like he's going to
sneeze. "Describe *what* for you?"

The Magnetron 2000 gets even longer and longer. I watch as its magnetic tip slowly attaches itself to . . . *a ring of keys* in the center of the Chief Historian's desk. This move is so bold that I am flabbergasted, stunned, astonished, confounded, stupefied, shocked, blown over, dazed, and literally beside myself. But I cannot lose my cool. My only job at the moment is to buy time for Milton.

Please describe the crash. There are so many kinds of mysterious crashes. It would help for me to know which kind this one was.

The Chief Historian frowns.

I will *not* describe it.

Milton carefully and quietly retracts the Magnetron 2000.

Because . . . you don't know enough adjectives?

I know *plenty* of adjectives!

Milton carefully and quietly removes the ring of keys from the magnet.

Excellent. I would love to hear at least *seven*.

The Chief Historian is outraged but refuses to shrink from the challenge.

Loud . . . sudden . . . surprising . . . brief . . .

Milton carefully and quietly creeps to the door at the far corner of the room.

. . . jangling . . . cacophonous . . . *unsuspicious!*

he concludes, with the opposite of unsuspicion.

Milton is trying the various keys, looking for the one that fits the lock.

NO. NOPE. NYET. NAH. UH-UH.

What caused the crash?

A toppling pile of tambourines.

And who caused them to topple?

No one! Piles of things sometimes topple all on their own.

I guess you must have stacked them badly.

The Chief Historian does not like this explanation.

I *always* stack *everything* extremely well!

If that's the case, then *someone* must have toppled them. Which suggests that there actually *was* an intruder.

The Chief Historian stands there looking like someone who has been caught with one hand in the COOKIE JAR and the other in a MOUSE TRAP.

"There was *no intruder*! When the police arrived, everything was in perfect order. Not a single file was missing! Which is why the case is *closed*!"

While the Chief Historian bellows like an elephant with an earache, Milton finds the right key and unlocks the door and disappears through it.

The Chief Historian puffs up his chest and blows his nose.

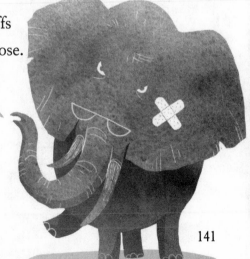

Now, if you will excuse me, I have *official* local-history business to attend to. I do not have time to talk to a *nosy little girl*.

141

Chief Historian Bernard Buxton has just used three words he doesn't seem to understand the meaning of, and I am forced to give him a Vocabulary Lesson.

First of all, I am not *nosy*.
I am *inquisitive*
and *thorough*.
I am a *detective*!

I say, like a chain saw explaining how things work to the trunk of a tree.

Furthermore, I am not *little*. I am in the eighty-third percentile for weight and the ninety-seventh percentile for height, and I have a head circumference that falls beyond the upper limit of the growth chart! And finally, while I may be a *girl*, I am also a *person*. And even though I am a *female* person, I am extremely *confident*, *strong*, and *capable*!

Perhaps you haven't heard, but GIRLS CAN DO ANYTHING!

Chief Historian Bernard Buxton looks like a planet that just got pummeled by an asteroid. He knows it's not okay to tell a proud fourth-grade girl she is incapable of greatness, and so he bites his tongue while his mind says all sorts of things I'm not allowed to hear.

It's probably time for me to leave, but Milton has not yet returned from wherever he went, and I need to buy him more time.

And so I ask a question that's been burning a hole in my curiosity.

"Chief of . . . *who*?"

"*Excuse* me?" As I hoped, I have the Chief Historian's undivided attention.

"Usually when someone is the *chief* of something, there are other people who they are the boss of. I assume there must be at least a dozen other historians here who look up to you because

YOU ARE SUCH A WISE AND CARING CHIEF.

Where are they?"

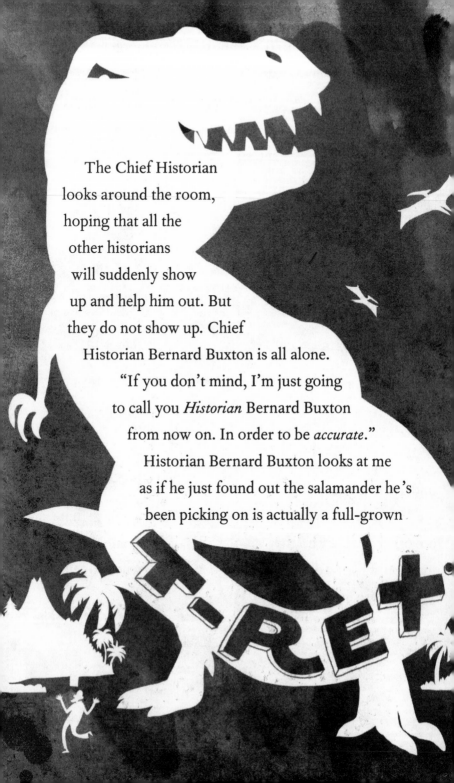

The Chief Historian
looks around the room,
hoping that all the
other historians
will suddenly show
up and help him out. But
they do not show up. Chief
Historian Bernard Buxton is all alone.

"If you don't mind, I'm just going
to call you *Historian* Bernard Buxton
from now on. In order to be *accurate*."

Historian Bernard Buxton looks at me
as if he just found out the salamander he's
been picking on is actually a full-grown

At that moment, Milton reappears and quietly scampers around the far side of Columbus to stand by my side. He appears to be holding something behind his back.

I don't know about you, Milton, I say, but I have all the information I need.

As do I, says Milton with a gleam in his eye.

Oh, look, he says, pointing to the floor.

Someone dropped his keys.

As Chief-of-No-Other-Historians Bernard Buxton puzzles over how his keys made their way across the room, I give my best "HARRUMPH!" and leave him standing there with neither children nor anyone else to boss around.

The moment we get outside, my actual interrogation begins.

"Where did you go? What did you find? *How could you be so bold?!*"

Milton grins like he just won a weight-lifting competition.

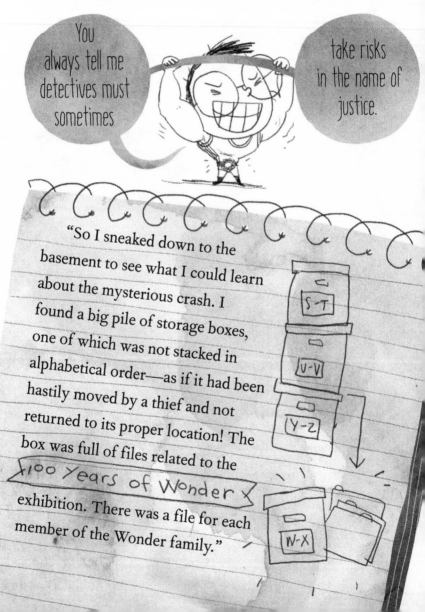

You always tell me detectives must sometimes

take risks in the name of justice.

"So I sneaked down to the basement to see what I could learn about the mysterious crash. I found a big pile of storage boxes, one of which was not stacked in alphabetical order—as if it had been hastily moved by a thief and not returned to its proper location! The box was full of files related to the 100 Years of Wonder exhibition. There was a file for each member of the Wonder family."

S-T

U-V

Y-Z

W-X

Milton hands me a Family Tree.

"Whose file do you think should have been between the files for Upchurch Wonder and Wendell Wonder?"

His eyes look as excited as I feel.

My brain scans the alphabet.

There's only one letter between *U* and *W*.

 Is *Veronica* Wonder one of *the* Wonders?

I ask.

 I think so! And according to the family tree,

Wendell and Upchurch are her cousins.

But her file wasn't in the box.

My brain kicks into overdrive. "Right before you went downstairs, the Chief Historian told me that 'not a single file was out of place' when the police arrived."

"But that's definitely not true!"

"Which means he's . . .

 ...LYING *to the* POLICE!"

147

Milton hands me a photograph of a teenage boy and girl with funny clothes and old-fashioned haircuts.

"I found this wedged between Upchurch's and Wendell's files," he says. "It must have fallen out when Veronica's was removed."

"Who are they?"

"Look closer," says Milton.

I look closer. The man looks *kind of* like . . . but it *can't* be . . . but maybe it *is*!

Mr. SHINE?!

"I think so!" says Milton. "And is that Veronica?"

NO WAY, I say.

The girl has big glasses and a frumpy dress and wild, frizzy hair. She looks nervous and uncertain and nothing like the Veronica I know. But there *is* something familiar about her eyes. If you took away the glasses . . . and added a blue sash.

I try to turn back time to see whether the powerful, confident superwoman I know as Veronica Wonder could *possibly* have ever looked like this.

I think it is her,

I say as my mind races to catch up with everything that's happened in the last few minutes.

1. Milton did something . . . daring.

2. It seems there definitely was a break-in at the Local House of History.

3. The Chief Historian is trying his hardest to cover it up.

4. The stolen file is somehow connected to Veronica.

5. Veronica is somehow connected to Mr. Shine.

Milton was right about something.

You did good, I say.

Milton glows like the firefly king.

As he should. My fearful little sidekick of a brother did something that was not only **AMAZING** but also

COMPLETELY AGAINST the RULES.

My heart roars with pride, and I'm tempted to lick the side of his face the way a mother lion would lick her newborn cub—before stopping myself, realizing how very, very weird that would be.

And then I remember that Milton owes me a theory.

"Tell me. How are the Dublingers duping each other?"

"Where do the eggs come from?" he asks.

I'm not sure, but Tracy is the one who fetched the ingredients.

Well, you should find out. Maybe Tracy is messing with the eggs.

Of course! How diabolical! And how is Tammy sabotaging Tracy?

Well, if Tracy's compass works fine, then maybe Tammy did something to her map.

Milton, you're a genius!

Milton blushes.

Like I said, it's just a theory.

But Milton's theory leaves us much further along in the Wonder Scouts case than we are when it comes to the

----Case of the Missing File----

I stare at the photo in my hands. Although it seems like an extremely important clue, we have no idea what caused those tambourines to topple or what the Chief Historian is hiding. Or who might want to steal Veronica's file.

Luckily, I know someone who probably does.

CHAPTER 9: RONNIE COLLINS

I've never been so eager for a Monday morning. When we get to school, I race to my classroom, where Mr. Shine is busy writing a list of *synonyms for cold.*

I do not waste a moment on cheerful hellos. There simply isn't time.

I have urgent business!

But Mr. Shine will not be rushed. He turns and smiles and bows his head slightly in greeting. "And good morning to you, Moxie."

"What do you make of this?" I ask, holding up the photo as if it were on fire.

At first he just squints at it. And then he smiles like the Grand Canyon splitting the unsuspecting desert of Arizona.

Where in the world did you get this?

he asks, gazing at the photo the way one might marvel at a chick poking out of its shell.

Look at us. Good old Ronnie.

"Ronnie?"

"Ronnie Collins. She's a girl I knew when I was younger. I told you about her. She's the one I used to practice foreign languages with. She went to private school, but we knew each other from

Wait . . . Ronnie is a girl? And what is Junior Historians?

It was a club run through the Local House of History.

"What do you remember about her?"

"Oh, she was quiet and shy. A little unsure. We both loved reading . . . and good stories. She moved away after high school, and I haven't seen her since."

153

"Well, she's back.
She's my Wonder Scout leader."
Mr. Shine's eyes grow wide.
"You mean your *Veronica* is . . . ?"
". . . your *Ronnie*."
"It sounds like she's changed quite a bit."
"She sure has. She's spent the past fifteen years traveling the world, seeking adventure and fortune. When she got back to Tiddlywhump, she started the evil organization known as the WONDER SCOUTS."

"I had no idea!"

Something confuses me. "You said her name was Ronnie . . . *Collins*?"

"That's right. But her great-grandmother's last name was Wonder."

"*Julia* Wonder?"

"Exactly."

"I wonder why she changed it."

Mr. Shine smiles. "Have you ever changed something about yourself?"

I think about that.

Back in Kindergarten, I wanted to be a unicorn, so I wore my hair in a single ponytail right in the middle of my head. But I don't do that anymore.

Obviously.

"So, why did you make the change?"

"Because pigtails feel more like me."

"*Exactly.* I'm guessing that as she got older, my old friend felt less like a Ronnie and more like a Veronica. She never seemed quite comfortable in her own skin."

I think about that line in the Wonder Scout Credo:

You have the power to change your own story.

Suddenly, it makes sense. Ronnie Collins was a nervous, quiet bookworm when she was growing up. And then she went out and traveled the world and got a new name in the process.

I guess she wanted to change her story.

I guess so.

Mr. Shine pauses.

Tell me what she's like now.

She's strong and smart. She always knows just what to say and just what to do. She's full of good advice.

That doesn't sound like someone who's in charge of an **EVIL** ORGANIZATION.

I know. It's very confusing. She gives me some hope for the Wonder Scouts.

Frankly, she sounds amazing.

I think about that. It's hard to disagree.

All day, I think about Veronica. All throughout the meeting that night, I look at her differently, trying to see her as the mousy, big-haired, glasses-wearing goofball in that photo.

But I can't.

She's  **STRONG,** teaching us what it means to be a self-confident woman who won't be pushed around by anyone.

She's  **KIND,** trying to coax Henrietta out of her shell.

She's  **PATIENT,** putting up with the Dublingers and their nonsense and trying her hardest to make them less awful.

There's nowhere she hasn't been.

There's nothing she hasn't seen.

There's no challenge she hasn't overcome.

The meeting is winding down. "Because of the camping trip on Friday, we'll do this week's badge challenges on Wednesday," says Veronica. "So practice up!"

I try not to notice that she's looking directly at me when she says this.

As the other girls head out front to wait for their parents, I stay behind with Veronica, trying to come up with something to talk to her about. I remember that Mom always says you can't go wrong by paying someone a compliment.

That was an extremely impressive story about your victory at Kamakura,

I say.

After the lesson, Veronica told us how she'd won a battle with a master samurai, not by beating him with a sword but by challenging him to a game of Chinese chess, which he had no idea how to play, because he was Japanese.

You kind of remind me of my hero and mentor. I mean, one of my *two* primary heroes and mentors.

Oh? Who's that?

Annabelle Adams, Girl Detective, protector of justice, thwarter of malfeasance, doer of improbable deeds. Have you heard of her?

Veronica seems slightly DIZZY and I don't blame her. Annabelle is a lot to take in.

I have not,

she says after a pause.

But she sounds amazing. And who is your other . . . *primary* . . . hero and mentor?

"Maggie McCoy, entomologist extraordinaire, asker of important scientific questions, fearless discoverer of bugs. She might not be a world-famous detective, but she is a

Veronica's eyes are wide. "Please ask her to pop in and say hello the next time she drops you off. I like to meet remarkable women."

"I would love to introduce you, but right now she's under the ocean in a submarine, exploring the depths of a deep-sea trench."

"That must be rather lonely."

"Oh, she's with some other scientists."

"I meant, lonely for *you*."

Suddenly, all the missing of Mom that's been building inside me comes gushing out, and I feel like a parade float that just lost its plug. The parts of Veronica that are fierce and stern transform into parts that are soft and warm and kind. I find myself wishing that there was a badge for long, affirming hugs.

"She might not be here all the time," I say, "but I wouldn't trade her for any other mom in the world. She makes me want to do extraordinary things. And . . . for the record, so do you."

Veronica smiles a deep smile, and suddenly, I rediscover my inner Annabelle and am back to my fully inflated self.

Which gives me a delicious thought:

Veronica might know everything about the *real* world, but if she's never read Annabelle, she wouldn't have any idea if I were to borrow an obscure fact from *Annabelle*'s world.

"I know it's not a badge challenge night, but I've just thought of an obscure fact."

"Excellent!" says Veronica. "I'm all ears."

"Did you know that the blood of a Lower Barmonian swamp frog contains a poison so deadly it can kill a 530-pound sumo champion in less than two minutes—but *also* contains the main ingredient of the only antidote that can reverse the poison and *save* him?"

Veronica gets a hard-to-read expression on her face, like she wants to say something but also doesn't want to say it. I'm guessing it's the look of someone who is not used to being outsmarted by a ten-year-old.

I . . . did not know that, she admits.

How can I know for sure it's true?

The word

hangs like a thundercloud over this otherwise-sunny moment, and I realize what I've done.

I consider admitting to Veronica that the fact is only true in a fictional world, but I also want her to think I am the sort of person who knows wonderful things—just like my mom and she do.

Because . . . I read it in a book,

I say, smiling my most trustworthy smile and hoping with my fingers crossed that she will not ask me which book I am referring to.

Veronica pauses for a second before saying, "All right, then." She reaches into her pouch and pulls out a colorful triangle of embroidered glory. "Congratulations on earning your OBSCURE FACTS BADGE."

"Thanks!" I say, delighted to have suddenly DOUBLED the size of my badge collection, and relieved that my secret is safe. "Well, good night!"

"Good night, Moxie. See you Wednesday."

"You certainly will," I say, wondering if I might actually have *three* primary heroes and mentors.

CHAPTER 10: THE GREAT DON SILVIO

On Wednesday morning, Mr. Shine is talking to us about something. I can't tell you what it is, because every inch of my enormous brain is otherwise occupied. Ever since he noticed I was reading my guidebook during class, I have a new strategy for not getting caught while thinking deep thoughts about Wonder Scouts:

1. Look directly at Mr. Shine when he talks.

2. Smile constantly.

3. Laugh when everyone else laughs.

4. Nod occasionally to show how hard I'm listening.

> Is it possible that Tracy is giving Tammy bad eggs? I wish Milton could come to the meeting and examine them himself.

The class laughs, so I laugh.

> Is there something wrong with Tracy's map? Milton would be so good at figuring out what it might be.

The class laughs some more, louder this time. So I laugh some more, louder this time. I nod my head a few times. This new plan is working beautifully.

Is it possible that Tammy is just really bad at making meringue and Tracy can't read a map to save her life?

Ooh! I like this theory best.

I laugh and nod my head. The rest of the class does neither.

"What's so funny, Moxie?" asks Mr. Shine.

Whether or not it's a great idea, I say the thing that's in my head at the moment.

Orienteering.

Orienteering? Why don't you tell the class what that is?

Using a map and a compass to navigate from

⊙ one place

to

⊙ another.

It's fun and pretty easy to learn.

Although, strangely, *some* people can't seem to figure out how to do it, no matter how hard they try.

It is too bad that there isn't a badge for MURDEROUS GLARING because Tracy would win it in a heartbeat.

I can't tell, but it looks like Tammy might be giving me a high five with her invisible third hand.

"What's so funny about orienteering?"

"Orienteering isn't funny at all," I say.

"It's EXTREMELY SERIOUS.

"I see," says Mr. Shine. "Thanks for that informative digression, Moxie, but do you have anything to add about *equivalent fractions*?"

"They definitely aren't funny, either."

The class laughs, but Mr. Shine gives me a look that he doesn't pull out very often. It's an

I'm pretty much running out of patience with you, Moxie,

kind of look.

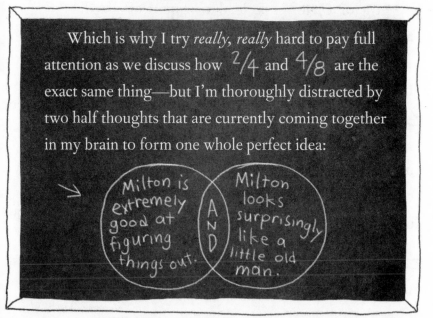

Which is why I try *really, really* hard to pay full attention as we discuss how $2/4$ and $4/8$ are the exact same thing—but I'm thoroughly distracted by two half thoughts that are currently coming together in my brain to form one whole perfect idea:

Milton is extremely good at figuring things out.

AND

Milton looks surprisingly like a little old man.

At recess, I remind Milton how good he is at figuring things out. I do not mention his resemblance to a little old man.

Why, thank you,

he says, puffing his feathers like a proud little finch before eyeing me suspiciously and adding,

What are you up to?

"*Up* to? *Up* to?" I pretend to be quite offended. "I'm just trying to pay my brother a compliment."

Milton seems not quite satisfied with my explanation, so I sit there for a moment, giving my kind words a chance to work their Magic.

"As much as I appreciate your exciting new theories about the Dublinger double cross, it would be far better if you could observe their badge challenges *in person*."

Milton is eating my praise like ice cream.

But how could I?

"If you were to go *undercover*, you could infiltrate the Wonder Scouts meeting and have a firsthand look."

"Undercover as what?" I can tell that Milton is 90% horrified but also maybe 10% excited about the idea.

"The possibilities are endless! You could be a

seal trainer

or a fighter pilot

or a real estate tycoon."

Milton is looking at me like I am missing the majority of my marbles.

"But . . . I was thinking you might be best suited to dress up as . . . a little old deliveryman from Tiddlywhump's favorite pizza restaurant, Looper's."

I can tell that Milton is tipping dangerously close to a NO,

and so I continue. "You once told me you'd do *whatever it takes* to crack a case. Did you mean it or not?"

Milton considers, the story of his thoughts unfolding on

his face. For a while, the plot is moving along pleasantly,

and I like my chances, but then it takes an unpleasant turn,

and I see him losing nerve. The gears in Milton's head start

grinding twice as fast as gears should, and I worry that they

might actually overheat, when he smiles and says,

I would *absolutely* do it except that it would be *impossible* to explain to Dad why I was dressed up like a little old pizza man and going to Wonder Scouts with you.

I hadn't thought about Dad. I'll have to come up with a whole new plan.

Recess ends. But instead of learning "ALL ABOUT the DIGESTIVE SYSTEM" I pull out a sheet of paper and pretend to take notes about the complex inner workings of the small intestine while instead writing a letter to my client and sworn enemy.

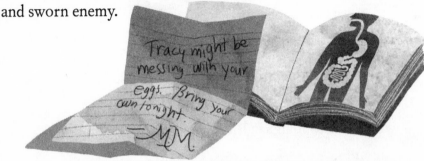

Tracy might be messing with your eggs. Bring your own tonight.
—MM

We get home and discover an absolute miracle: a note from Dad. The answer to my prayers.

"*Mil*ton," I sing with a booming delight that would surely ring the Wonder Bell, "time to get your *cos*tume on!"

Milton reads the note.

Hey M&M—
Looks like I'll have to work late tonight. (The state of Alabama ran out of bicycles!). Can Milton tag along and read in the corner during Moxie's meeting? And can one of Emily's dads take you to Wonder Scouts?
—Dad ♡

171

NOOOOOOO! says Milton with an equally booming despair.

But it's too late. I've already found the hat I won by eating a Super Looper with all the toppings in less than 5 minutes.

I'm already pulling out the old-man wig and mustache from the time I was Albert Einstein for Halloween.

No matter that I added some *silver glitter* for extra excitement. No matter that more than a few of the hairs have fallen out, leaving some bald spots.

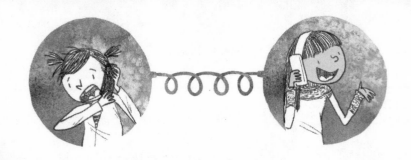

I call Emily to ask for a ride to Wonder Scouts, and then I order a Quadrooper Looper.

Our pizza arrives with just a minute to spare before one of Emily's dads (I can never remember his name) arrives to pick us up.

It's Jim, he says as we get in the car, in response to the question on my face.

Hello, Jim! I say.

Thank you for giving us a ride.

Which is when I realize I should probably explain why Milton is dressed as a little old man and carrying an enormous pizza.

It's . . . Bring Your Little Brother to Wonder Scouts Night,

I say, realizing that this only explains why Milton is in the car, but not why he's dressed like a little old pizza man.

Jim gives me a look like he's waiting for the rest of the story.

It's also . . . Dress Like Your favorite Character from a Book Night,

I say,

and Milton is dressed up as . . .

the great . . .

Don Silvio.

I'm not sure why this particular name comes to mind, except that it is the name of the priest from chapter 7 of Annabelle Adams, Girl Detective, Volume 22:

Pi Squared, in which Annabelle thwarts the irrational marriage of the Duke of Diameter (Fungo in disguise!) to the Countess of Circumference as the clock strikes 3:14 p.m.

Milton scowls, and I can't say I blame him.

"What book is Don Silvio from?" asks Jim.

"*A Tale of Two Pizzas*," I say, thinking fast.

"I see," says Jim. "And who are you supposed to be?"

I look down at my shirt and pants, searching the library shelves of my mind for someone or anyone at all I might happen to look like.

But there's only one best answer to his question.

Moxie McCoy,

I say with a confident nod.

From the

AUTOBIOGRAPHY of MOXIE McCOY,

which I haven't yet written but plan to someday.

Jim says absolutely nothing at all. We drive for a few minutes, Milton fuming, Jim quietly shaking his head, me counting the streetlights.

"Please drop us by the back door, if you don't mind," I say to Jim. "Don Silvio wants to make a

with his pizza."

We get out of the car and wave good-bye to Jim. He seems to be waiting for us to go inside, but I just keep waving. When he finally drives off, Milton heads for the bushes. I put on my headband and glasses and run around front, heart already pounding, wondering how in the world we're going to pull this off.

CHAPTER 11: LOUD ENOUGH TO RING THE WONDER BELL

The meeting begins with the song and then the Credo. When it looks like we might be getting ready to start the challenges, I casually wander over to

the window and give a long, dramatic, full-bodied yawn complete with jazz hands, which is the signal Milton and I have agreed on.

Is everything all right, Moxie?

Veronica sounds a little irritated and a little concerned.

Oh yes. I'm fine. I spent so much time practicing for tonight's badge challenges that I got a bit sleepy.

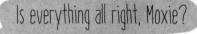

All right,

says Veronica.

Could you please come back and join us in the circle?

At that moment, a little old man with an extremely large  **PIZZA BOX** walks into the room.

Hello there,

says Veronica.

Can I help you?

Yes,

says Milton.

But that's all he says as he continues to stand there awkwardly. His arms start to *TREMBLE,* and I'm worried he might drop the pizza.

I'm Veronica.

I'm . . .

And that's where Milton gets the look that means his brain is on vacation. Which happens sometimes when it's asked to do too much. I know I need to help it find its way home.

SEE YA! WOULDN'T WANNA BE YA!

"Hey!" I say, leaping into action. "I know you! You're that pizza deliveryman from Looper's. Your name is . . ."

While Veronica and all the other Wonder Scouts wait for me to finish my sentence, my brain goes on vacation, too, and I can't come up with *one single other name* from the *thousands of names available*. I look at Veronica. She looks at me.

OH, Hey

It's like all of time and space has stopped and I am suspended in a great vat of chilly, dark emptiness where no memories are allowed.

But finally, from the tiniest, darkest back cupboard of my mind,

like a golden rope of hope and light, I remember.

"DON SILVIO,"

I say—

at the exact same moment that Milton, in a perfectly convincing little-old-pizza-deliveryman accent says,

"RON".

A jolt of displeasure awakens Milton from his daze. He gives me the deepest scowl.

"Yes . . . Ron . . . Don Silvio," he says. "I've come to deliver the pizza."

"Hello . . . Ron Don Silvio," says Veronica without missing a beat. Then she turns to us. "Did someone order pizza?" Of course, none of us raise our hands.

"I'm sorry," says Veronica to Ron Don Silvio. "There must be some mistake."At which point, Milton turns to leave.

Which must not happen!

"*I* ordered the pizza," I say, waving my right hand with a grand flourish.

"You *did*?" asks Veronica suspiciously.

"Yes!" I say, waving my *left* hand with an even grander flourish. "Badge challenges consume so much of our precious energy that I thought we could use a nutritious snack. I wanted it to be a surprise, so . . .

SURPRISE!"

181

Thank you, says Veronica, looking at Milton with her microscope gaze.

Did your . . . *father* drive you here tonight?

I swoop in before Milton can mess things up,

Oh no. Ron Don Silvio's *father* is 97 years old and can no longer drive. He spends his evenings playing bingo.

Veronica looks at me like I have two heads. The Wonder Scouts chatter and giggle to themselves. These are strange happenings.

"I'll just put the pizza over here," says Ron Don Silvio.

"Thank you," says Veronica, clearly waiting for him to leave. But Ron Don Silvio does not leave. Instead, he opens the pizza box and, as we discussed, starts cutting the pizza into tiny squares.

"Thank you, but you can go now," says Veronica as politely as she can.

"Haven't you heard?" I say, pleading with my eyes for Milton to keep playing along. "Looper's now offers an extra-special service! Their little old deliverymen cut your pizza into handy, bite-sized servings!"

"How . . . nice," says Veronica, clearly exasperated but also ready to move on with the meeting.

While Milton cuts pizza with the speed and vigor of an arctic slug,

THAT'S COLD MAN!

Veronica does her best to continue.

Because we'll be camping this Friday, we're going to do our badge challenges this evening. Who would like to—

Master Baker!

says Tammy, waving her hand like a hatchet.

I look over at Milton to make sure he's paying attention. Both of us watch as the Dublinger drama unfolds.

"*I'll* get the supplies," says Tracy. But this time, instead of protesting, Tammy waits patiently while Tracy gathers the mixer and bowl and ingredients.

"Thank you, *sister*. But I brought my own EGGS this time," says Tammy with a sly smile as she pulls a carton of eggs from her backpack.

Tracy gasps. Veronica looks puzzled. "Is there something wrong with the other eggs?"

"That's an excellent question," says Tammy. "We're about to find out." With that, she separates and mixes the eggs she brought. We wait and watch and whisper with excitement. For a thrilling moment, it looks like the meringue is finally going to work. But then, just as quickly, it dissolves into a dismal EGGY SOUP.

"ARRRRGHH!" Tammy is unhinged.

I'm torn between enjoying the fate of an unhappy Dublinger and feeling like I'm failing my client.

 says Tracy's face.

 Poor Tammy, says Hilly.

Hmmm, says Ron Don Silvio, while watching the proceedings and yanking on his earlobe like his life depends on it.

Veronica glances over to see how the pizza cutting is coming along, and Milton dives back to work.

Veronica's attention returns to the circle when Tracy announces her intention to challenge for the Orienteering badge. "But," says Tracy, while shooting Tammy a glass-shattering glare, "I'd prefer to use someone *else's* map."

"All right," says Veronica, who seems increasingly aware that something strange is going on. "Whose would you like to use?"

"Yours," says Tracy.

"Of course," says Veronica, taking out her map and handing it to Tracy, who grabs her compass and

 SPRINTS OUT THE DOOR.

As eager as I am to find out whether a different map will make a difference for Tracy, I'm also ready to put all my practice to the test. "While Tracy is out orienteering, I'd like to challenge for the Pig Latin badge."

"Very well," says Veronica. "Atwhay etsgay iggerbay ethay oremay ouyay aketay awayway?"

I hadn't realized that Veronica was going to jump right into it. At first my brain resists, but then it relaxes and lets the strange sounds flow through it like water through a spaghetti drainer.

Suddenly I know without thinking that Veronica has said: "What gets bigger the more you take away?"

Which makes me panic because the question makes no sense. But then I remember that *seeming* to make no sense is what makes a riddle a riddle and that the fun happens when you wiggle your way through the BOG of CONFUSION and discover the entirely sensible explanation on the other side.

Once I remind myself that every riddle has a solution, I ask my inner Annabelle what *she* would do in this situation. To which she replies, "Moxie, might I remind you of Volume 41:

The Hole Enchilada,

in which my nemesis, Dr. Fungo, opens a Mexican restaurant right next door to an extremely fancy bank and forces his employees to spend their lunch hour using brittle plastic spoons to dig a tunnel that grows longer and longer as they remove the dirt and rocks?"

Which is how I know for an *absolute fact* that the only thing that increases in size as you remove things from it is

says Veronica, reaching into her
pouch and handing me the

"Oorayhay!" says Hilly.
"*OOOOO-BAY!*" say Tammy
Dublinger's vicious frowning eyebrows.

Just then Tracy comes back with an
angry ocelot where her face should be.

"Here," she says, handing Veronica
the map. "This one doesn't work, either."
Veronica frowns. "When you're
struggling with something, it's important
not to place the blame elsewhere, Tracy."
Tracy's look makes it clear that she knows *exactly* where
she'd like to place the blame, but that, for now at least, she
can't prove Tammy's guilt.
Ron Don Silvio's eyes are glued to Tracy.
His brain is clearly working double time.

Perhaps inspired by Tracy's despair and against my better judgment, I stand up and say, "I'd like to challenge for Polyglot."

"Are you *sure* you're ready this time?" asks Veronica.

"Yes," I say. I am not *quite* sure, but I *want* to be sure. I did *pretty* well with my practice last night. It's true that I never got through *all seven* languages without making a mistake, but I was *close.*

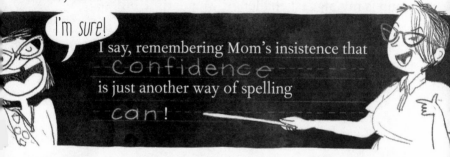

I'm SURE! I say, remembering Mom's insistence that confidence is just another way of spelling can!

"All right, then," says Veronica. "Let's start with Spanish."

I count to ten in Spanish without breaking a sweat. Soon Portuguese, Russian, Hindi, and Bengali are also safely behind me.

I stumble a bit as I tiptoe through my Arabic

but somehow make it safely to the end.

Suddenly, all that stands between me and the promised land is my biggest challenge, Mandarin Chinese.

I push forward, undaunted.

"*Yī, èr, sān . . .*"

Everyone's eyes are on me.

" . . . *sì, wǔ, liù . . .*"

The **TENSION** is so **THICK** you could spread it on a piece of bread and make a decent sandwich.

And TASTY!

" . . . *qī . . . bā . . .*"

I am two syllables shy of Polyglot glory . . . but that's where my memory fails me.

My mind is as empty as Santa's cookie plate on Christmas morning. Not even a crumb of an inkling of a snickerdoodle remains for me to latch onto.

All my confidence was not *quite* enough. I am prepared to admit defeat. But at that moment, Ron Don Silvio sneezes.

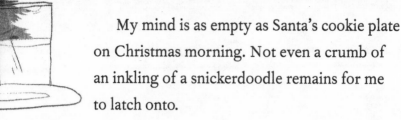

"HA-JIŬ!"

It is a strange sort of sneeze, but Ron Don Silvio is not your average pizza deliveryman.

Suddenly, for whatever reason, the sneeze clears the cotton from my head, and I suddenly remember *out of absolutely nowhere* that the way to say "nine" in Mandarin Chinese is . . .

"*Jiŭ!*"

And from there, I am able to easily climb the final step to "ten," which is *shí!*

The Wonder Scouts burst into applause. "Well *done!*" says Veronica, handing me a badge. "We have a brand-new Polyglot in our midst!"

Tracy points at me with a look of stunned outrage on her face.

But . . . she cheated.

What do you mean?

asks Veronica, offended by the suggestion.

The pizza man gave her the answer.

EXCUSE ME?!

Milton is also outraged.

You CHEATED You CHEATING CHEATER!

Tracy sneers, putting her nose way closer to mine than is legal in the nation of Moxie.

Veronica is *NOT AMUSED.*

That's enough, Tracy!

But I don't need Veronica to fight this battle for me.

WHAT DID YOU SAY?

You heard me.

Like a stock car rumbling at the starting line as the race is about to begin, my engine purrs with white-hot rage.

I stare at Tracy Dublinger like a bat stares at a baseball, like an arrow stares at its target, like a bowling ball stares at those ten helpless pins.

Tracy stares back. It is a dark, deep, smoldering, before-the-dawn-of-time kind of stare. We have climbed into the ring, and only one of us is going to step out alive.

"Ooh! It's a staring contest!" says Megan Lacey.

"Give them space," says Veronica.

The other Scouts form a circle around Tracy and me as we settle in for the battle.

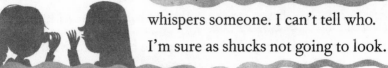

Tracy is the defending champion, whispers someone. I can't tell who. I'm sure as shucks not going to look.

. . . so a *badge* is on the line, says someone else.

I have never looked directly at Tracy Dublinger for this many seconds in a row, and it is even more unpleasant than I could have imagined. Her angry eyebrows twitch in a disconcerting way. Her beady eyes quiver like a geyser preparing to blow. Her

HOT, minty BREATH

wafts oppressively into my airspace, and I find myself grateful that Tracy is so devoted to brushing her teeth.

In response, I pull out Annabelle's patented

I start with a **3 out of 10** and slowly increase the intensity to a *full* **9.8**

I can see Tracy's resolve start to crumble as she beholds the wonder of my ferocity. If I can hold out a few seconds longer, victory will be mine. But Tracy is not the defending champion by accident.

She digs down into her own arctic well, sharpening the fury of her angry serpent eyes, flaring the edges of her sharp little nostrils, and nearly knocking me backward with her

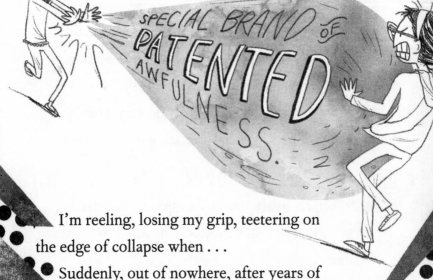

SPECIAL BRAND OF PATENTED AWFULNESS.

I'm reeling, losing my grip, teetering on the edge of collapse when . . .

Suddenly, out of nowhere, after years of painful failure, my right eyebrow finally obeys my endless pleas and rises into a

high, proud, devastating arch.

I can feel it happening. My only regret is that I cannot behold my own glory.

There is a moment of deafening tension followed by the thrilling swell of victory as Tracy wilts like a flower that has suffered too long in the noonday sun.

Her body slumps. She turns away. There is an interesting moment in which Tammy walks over as if she's going to comfort her sister but then changes her mind.

My view of the Dublingers is eclipsed by the ring of cheering Scouts that surrounds me. Tracy has been dethroned! Darkness has been vanquished by light!

Congratulations, Moxie, on winning the staring contest!

says Veronica, reaching into her pouch.

197

At least I'm not a *cheater,*

mumbles Tracy, technically under her breath but still loudly enough for all of us to hear.

Her words light the **DYNAMITE** that has been piling up inside me throughout the past few minutes of bone-biting tension.

"MOXIE McCOY DOES NOT CHEAT!!"

Everyone is so stunned and silent that you *should* have been able to hear a pin drop. Except you can't . . . because the WONDER BELL is RINGING.

No one knows whether to look up or down, whether to cringe or laugh, whether to feel sorry for Tracy or to congratulate me. Veronica breaks the silence.

Congratulations, Moxie, on *also* earning the Loudest Yell badge,

she says, reaching into her pouch yet again.

Tracy Dublinger looks as if she would probably tear out her hair in frustration . . . if only it weren't her most prized possession.

I glance over to share my triumph with Ron Don Silvio and notice that he is standing with crossed legs and a desperate expression.

I know that look. Milton has to pee.

I gesture with my eyes toward the hallway that leads to the bathrooms and watch as he scampers in that direction.

199

"Would you look at that!" I say. "The pizza is finally ready!"

The Scouts descend on the Quadrooper Looper, and I head down the hallway, impatient to find out what Milton has learned.

While I wait for him to come out of the bathroom, I look at the display case full of trophies from the community soccer league. I see myself reflected in the glass.

I seem so *wholesome* with my headband and glasses and sash.

That person *looks* like me and *feels* like me. I wonder if maybe she *is* me.

I am puzzling over the question when Milton comes out of the bathroom looking like an extremely unhappy little old man. But there's no time to worry about his feelings. I have to know what he's thinking.

So? Did you figure it out?

But Milton isn't interested in chitchat.

Maybe. I'm not sure. I want to leave.

If you're not sure, I need you to stay a bit longer. This is our best chance to figure out what the Dublingers are up to.

No, Moxie! I'm tired of pretending to be someone I'm not. Aren't *you*?

Yes! I am tired of wearing this disguise, but I'm not willing to give up when we're so close to putting an end to the Wonder Scouts once and for all!

I hear a *GASP* and see someone else reflected in the glass.

I turn, and there is Hilly, looking like a priceless vase that someone just knocked off its pedestal and is about to shatter on a cold stone floor. She turns to leave.

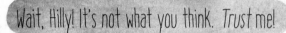

Wait, Hilly! It's not what you think. *Trust* me!

Trust you?

Her eyes are as angry as something on fire.

I don't even know who you *are!*

Hilly runs back down the hall, leaving me wishing there were something in the guidebook for what comes next.

When Milton and I get back to the meeting room, the other Scouts are getting ready to leave, and Hilly is nowhere to be seen. I go outside to find her, but she's already gone.

I don't have her phone number and don't even know where she lives. There is no way to explain myself. No way to apologize. No way to beg her to keep my secret.

I go back inside and find Veronica. Even though everything has fallen apart, I still need to show her my leaf project.

Impressive work, she says, thumbing carefully through my scrapbook of leaf samples before handing me my Arborist badge.

You've picked up so much in such a short time.

Thanks, I say, wishing I could enjoy the compliment.

What's the matter? asks Veronica, prying into my soul with her crowbar stare.

But I don't know what to say. So much is the matter in this moment.

Through the window, I see Dad pull up. "I have to go," I say. "And you'd probably better get back to Looper's, Ron Don Silvio. I bet they're wondering where you are."

Good night,

says Veronica, her eyes shining with love. She can tell that things are not quite okay.

And remember . . .

She trails off, waiting for me to finish.

Girls can do *anything.*

Even as I say the words, I'm finding it hard to believe them.

Veronica gives me a dignified nod. I try to give one of my own, but Milton is dragging me backward like a little old pizza man who is more than ready to take off his wig.

As soon as we're out of the building, Ron Don Silvio leaps behind a bush, does a quick change, and reappears a moment later as Milton again.

He doesn't notice, and I'm not going to point it out, but there is some silver glitter on his face. It sparkles like magic whenever we pass under a streetlamp.

It almost makes me feel better about the crumbling disaster that is my current reality. Almost.

CHAPTER 12: EVERYONE IS STILL A SUSPECT

On Thursday morning, my mind is full of questions I can't answer.

How can I explain myself to Hilly?

Will she ever forgive me?

Will she blow my cover?

Will she tell Veronica?

So instead of sitting here stewing, I keep my mind occupied by actually focusing on Mr. Shine's helpful advice about how to avoid run-on sentences, but then I decide I already know all about run-on sentences and would never use them ever in a million years so I get entirely bored and start thinking about Milton who was too mad to talk about the case when we got home last night and still wasn't feeling chatty at breakfast.

I find him during recess and demand answers.

"Out with it. What did you learn at the meeting?"

"There's something wrong with Tammy's bowl."

"Her *bowl*? What do you mean? It's a *bowl*."

If the eggs are fine and the mixer works, her bowl is the next most likely source of the problem.

"Do you have any idea *what* is wrong with the bowl?"

"Not yet. By the time I got a chance to take a closer look, it was an eggy mess."

"Well, did you figure out what Tammy is doing, at least?"

"Tracy used Veronica's map last night, so that can't be it. And we already knew her compass works fine. Maybe someone is moving the cache? Are you sure there's not a third Dublinger who is conspiring with Tammy?"

I am nearly knocked over by this horrifying thought. But I manage to go on.

"Is that all you've got?" I am doing a not-very-good job of hiding my disappointment.

"So far," says Milton, who is doing an even worse job of hiding his irritation.

"But do you at least believe the Dublingers are the only suspects?"

"As far as I'm concerned, *everyone* is still a suspect," he says, giving me a very unbrotherly scowl.

"Including Hilly." He gets up from the bench and gives me a stare.

I assume that Milton is joking as he says this, but he does not crack a smile as he walks over to the bench where he used to sit before we formed our agency.

I sit down and try to think things through. But only for a moment, because suddenly I am face-to-face with an agitated Dublinger.

It wasn't the eggs.

Tammy is in a mood.

Apparently not. Good theory, though, right?

Theories don't earn badges!

Detective work takes time.

I expect results!

So do I.

Tammy storms off with the perfect combination of indignation and poise that only a Dublinger could muster.

When school ends, Hilly is waiting outside, standing there with her arms folded, like the gates of a forbidding fortress. I barely have time to slip on my headband and glasses before she begins her interrogation.

What is your name?

Moxie Minerva McCoy.

Is that your *real* name?

Yes.

Do you actually hate soup?

I DO!

Hilly looks mildly comforted. It's my turn to ask a question.

Have you told anyone?

No. I like to know the facts *before* I start talking.

My heart soars with relief.

A good policy.

So tell me the facts.
What are you up to?

I look at Hilly and she looks at me. She is mad, she is smart, and she is not going to be convinced by anything but the entire truth. I decide to lay it all out and hope for the best.

I tell her that the Moxie McCoy she thinks she knows is but an illusion. That the 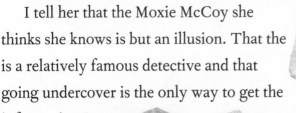 is a relatively famous detective and that going undercover is the only way to get the information I need to solve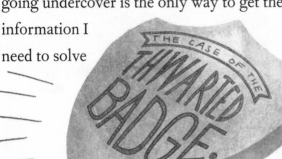

I can tell that Hilly is kind of impressed to be talking with someone who is technically a celebrity. "Okay, that *sort of* makes sense. But what was all that about you wanting to bring an end to the Wonder Scouts?"

I lean in close and whisper in Hilly's ear,

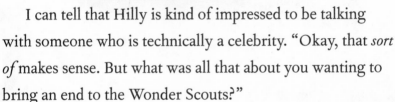

I hate to break it to you, but Wonder Scouts is a twisted and sinister organization bent on the corruption of young minds.

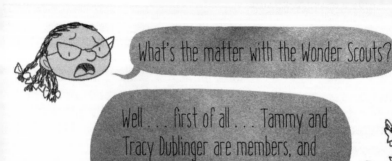

What's the matter with the Wonder Scouts?

Well . . . first of all . . . Tammy and Tracy Dublinger are members, and they are the absolute worst.

Okay . . .

what else?

Second, it's obvious that . . .

But that's as far as I get before my brain runs out of complaints.

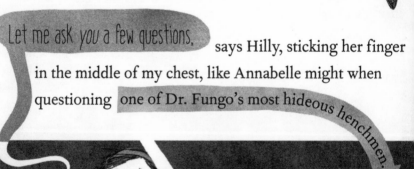

Let me ask *you* a few questions, says Hilly, sticking her finger in the middle of my chest, like Annabelle might when questioning one of Dr. Fungo's most hideous henchmen.

Have you gotten to know an amazing woman who has traveled the world doing amazing things and is now teaching us how to be amazing, too?

I cannot deny it.

Have you made a new friend who has spent *a lot of her time* trying to teach you stuff so you can earn your badges?

I absolutely have.

It is suddenly very important to me that Hilly know exactly how much I appreciate her friendship.

Do you think Veronica and I are *twisted and sinister*?

I absolutely don't!

Then why in the world would you want to put an end to the Wonder Scouts?

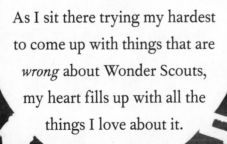

As I sit there trying my hardest to come up with things that are *wrong* about Wonder Scouts, my heart fills up with all the things I love about it.

213

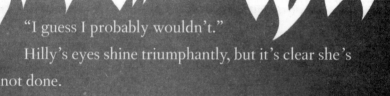

"I guess I probably wouldn't."

Hilly's eyes shine triumphantly, but it's clear she's not done.

"I *do* think it makes sense to investigate Tammy and Tracy. I *agree* it's weird that neither of them has been able to earn her final badge. If it turns out that they are up to no good, Veronica *should* know. But if you do a *single thing* to hurt the Wonder Scouts itself, so help me, Moxie Minerva McCoy, you will personally answer to Hildegard Gwenivere Jackson. Wonder Scouts is *extremely important* to me! And I thought it was important to *you*."

Her words burn like the sidewalk on bare feet in summer.

"It is!" I say, surprising myself by how much I mean it.

"One more question," says Hilly, glaring at me like a chicken might glare at a fried egg.

Is that your actual hairdo?

I take off my headband and restore my magnificent pigtails.

Hilly's scowl relaxes a little. "I like that *so* much better."

"Me TOO," I say, relieved.

"And the glasses?"

I take them off. "Better without?"

"Two hundred percent."

I stop a second and let it sink in. Hilly prefers the actual me to the undercover one. Though at the moment, it seems she's not terribly fond of either version.

For the record, I'm not quite ready to forgive you, and I'm still not sure when I will be.

With that, Hilly stomps off in a way that makes clear she doesn't want me to follow.

I stand there feeling as flat as a lid that someone just removed *from a* TUNA CAN. And just as jagged around the edges.

That night after dinner, Dad takes us shopping. He gets me my own flint so I can challenge for the Fire Starter badge on the camping trip, and, to be fair, he gets Milton some new batteries for his walkie-talkies.

When we get home, we play board games, and afterward Milton and I use the walkie-talkies to chat from our separate bedrooms.

I have a new theory in the Local House of History case,

he says.

Oh!

I say.

Tell me!

I'm so discouraged by the lack of progress on the Wonder Scouts front that I could really use some good news.

Well, I've racked my brain again and again, and the only person I can think of who could possibly want to steal Veronica's folder is . . .

Who?

I'm excited. When Milton has a theory, it's usually not wrong.

. . . Veronica.

I turn off the walkie-talkie and take the batteries out so there is zero chance it can come back on. Because what Milton just said is plain ridiculous.

I go downstairs and ask Dad if we can try calling Mom. Even though I know we won't get her, I want to hear her voice on the recording.

It rings a few times, but her message doesn't play. Instead, I hear, "Hello . . . Dale?"

Mom?

I say.

MOM! It's MOXIE!

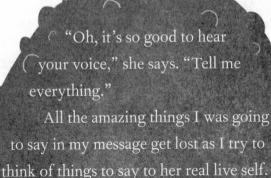

"Oh, it's so good to hear your voice," she says. "Tell me everything."

All the amazing things I was going to say in my message get lost as I try to think of things to say to her real live self.

"I'm good," I say. "I joined a new club. But I got myself into a bit of a pickle."

"You want to talk about it?"

"Not really. You already taught me exactly what I need to do to fix it."

"So you're going to be all right?"

"Absolutely."

"Promise?"

"Yeah."

"How's my little squeeze?" She's talking about Milton. "Are you looking out for him like I asked you to?"

"Of course!" I say. I do not mention that I have recently put him up to wearing an old-man wig and infiltrating a meeting for wholesome girls.

"You know what?" she says. I can tell Mom is ramping up to deliver some wise advice.

"What?"

"Even though they're kind of sour, pickles can be pretty delicious."

I laugh because she's right. They often are.

"I'll see you *really* soon," says Mom. But I know better than to ask exactly when she's coming home. She never knows for sure.

I pause for just a minute, enjoying the sound of her breathing.

"Now let me talk to Dad," she says. "I miss that guy."

"Okay," I say. My parents are goofy in love.

"I love you," she says.

I say it back. And then I say it back again.

I hand the phone to Dad and head up to my room, feeling not as bad about today and a whole lot better about tomorrow.

CHAPTER 13: ROUGHING IT

At first recess, Emily and I walk over to Milton's bench, where he is waiting with a question.

> If it wasn't Veronica herself, then who *would* want to steal her file?

My well-oiled detective mind leaps instantly to the likeliest explanation. "I bet it was Veronica's cousins. What were their names?"

"Upchurch and Wendell?"

"Yes. Sneaky names, if you ask me. I bet they are identical twins with bald heads and boring lives and extremely itchy bathrobes who are jealous of Veronica and don't want her to be included in the Julia Wonder exhibit because the details of her fabulous life would make them look so dull and unaccomplished!"

I am excited. That *has* to be it. But Milton is shaking his head.

You are basing that on nothing!

You are MAKING that UP!!

Milton is missing the point. A detective must consider *every* possibility. "Maybe I am, but it makes perfect sense! Have you come up with a better explanation?"

Milton looks like he'd rather eat a plate of baby porcupines than admit defeat. But then he yanks on his earlobe and says,

Not yet.

"What about the Chief Historian?" Emily suggests.

I like this theory! I'd love nothing more than to put the Chief of Absolutely No One

BEHIND BARS.

"He's clearly hiding something," says Milton. "But what would *his* motive be?"

"Perhaps *he* didn't want Veronica to be included in the exhibition," I say. "Because he's worried her bold deeds and accomplishments would

OVERSHADOW

Julia herself!"

"Maybe, but why would he pretend there was a break-in?" says Milton. "Why wouldn't he just throw away the files and be done with it?"

Milton makes an excellent point.

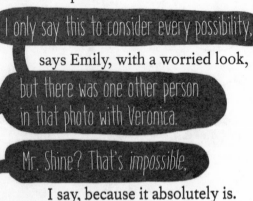

I only say this to consider every possibility,

says Emily, with a worried look,

but there was one other person in that photo with Veronica.

Mr. Shine? That's *impossible*,

I say, because it absolutely is.

The best criminals always make you think so,

says Milton.

After school, Dad drives me out to the base of Boo Mountain, where the Wonder Scouts are gathering for the camping trip. I have Dad's old sleeping bag and my flint and my stuffed chicken, Homer, who I've never slept without and never will.

As we hike around Stone Lake, Veronica tells us about the various plants and rocks and butterflies we see along the way. I surprise myself by already knowing the names of some of the trees.

Hilly is walking as far ahead of me as she can. As I try to catch up with her, she moves farther down the path, as if an invisible force field is keeping us apart.

Veronica shows us how to bait our hooks and cast our lines. I even catch a trout but don't enjoy it as much as I'd like to.

She shows us how to CUT THE FISH INTO FILLETS, which is kind of gross but also kind of fascinating.

"Now we need some way to cook it," she says with a playful gleam in her eye. "Who would like to challenge for the Fire Starter badge?"

Five of us raise our hands, including Hilly, who has tried during the past two camping trips to win this badge with the good old rubbing-two-sticks-together-as-fast-as-you-can technique but hasn't been able to make it work. Now she has a flint and is excited to try again.

The other Scouts form a circle and watch as the five of us gather our little piles of dry pine needles and prepare for the challenge.

READY... SET... GO!

We spring into action. I look to my right. Hilly has made a few good sparks but hasn't been able to get her pine needles to catch fire. Despite our fight, I'm rooting for her.

Tracy Dublinger leans over to get a good look at what Hilly is up to and . . .

spills her hot chocolate all over Hilly's hand and flint.

HEY!!

says Hilly.

"Ooops. *Sorry,*" says Tracy, with a face that says, *That was fun, and I'd do it again.*

"Veronica! Can we please stop so I can dry my flint?" Hilly is desperate. She knows a sticky, wet flint is not going to make any sparks.

"I'm sorry," says Veronica with the perfect blend of kindness and firmness, "but accidents happen. Surprises pop up. A Scout must be resourceful, come what may."

Hilly looks as crushed as a cantaloupe that just fell off a roof.

Ninety seconds left!

says Veronica.

Here,

I say, handing my flint to Hilly.

What? Why?

Take it,

I say.

I've got these.

I pick up two sticks to show her that it's no big deal.

Hilly's face melts from anger into gratitude, and my heart bobs up like a leaky old bath toy that suddenly remembered how to float. "Thank you!"

"Let's *do* this!" I say, smiling.

I grab my two sticks and rub them together like the string and bow of an excitable fiddler. But there are no sparks.

"Sixty seconds left," says Veronica.

  says Megan Lacey as her pine needles leap into flame.

I'm getting exactly nowhere with my sticks, so I grab two others, but these are even soggier than the first two.

 says Henrietta Bork.

"*Excellent* job, Henrietta!" says Veronica. "Thirty seconds left."

Hilly is still working away with my flint, making sparks that have not yet caught, and I wonder if I've made a terrible mistake. It would be such a waste if *neither* of us earned the badge.

I start to panic. If I don't get this badge today, I won't be able to try again until the next camping trip, which might not be for a month or more.

I'm feeling very sorry for myself, when I remember Annabelle Adams, Girl Detective, Volume 26: *Roughing It*, in which the 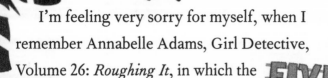 **FIVE-STAR HOTEL** where Annabelle is doing a stakeout is evacuated because of a faulty sprinkler system, and Annabelle and the other guests have to spend the night in the jungle instead.

Everything is so damp that no one can start a fire in the usual way, so Annabelle goes about it in a very *un*usual way.

Hoping against hope, I reach into my sweatshirt pocket, and, *yes*, the walkie-talkie batteries are still there.

"Hilly, may I have a piece of gum?" I ask, not wanting to waste even a fraction of a second on pleasantries. "It's an emergency!"

Without skipping a beat, Hilly slides a pack of gum out of her pocket and TOSSES ME A STICK, which I catch with one hand and unwrap in a single deft move.

Ten seconds, says Veronica.

Using the metallic part of the wrapper to connect the battery's terminals, I create a spark, which lands on the pine needles and causes them to smolder. I blow lightly on the embers, and an enthusiastic flame appears.

GOT IT!

It is the most exciting moment of my whole entire life.

"Very nice, Moxie," says Veronica. "What a fascinating technique."

"Thanks," I say. "I just invented it on the spot." As the words come out of my mouth, I have a slightly UNCOMFORTABLE feeling, like I just put on someone else's shirt, and it doesn't quite fit.

GOT IT!

says Hilly, her eyes bright with excitement.

I smile at Hilly, and she smiles at me, and now *this* is the most exciting moment in my whole entire life.

Poor Bonnie Groff does not seem to have gotten it.

She is rubbing her two sticks together so slowly and gently that I'm surprised they haven't fallen asleep.

TIME'S UP!!

says Veronica.

"It seems we have *four* new  in our midst. And . . ."
Veronica pauses and looks at me with eyes so kind and loving that I almost fall over. "I've decided to award Moxie the badge for lending Hilly her flint in the middle of the challenge. I consider that an act of *true* friendship."

Like opposite ends of a seesaw, Tracy's mouth drops into a wretched frown as mine rises into a delighted grin.

"That's a *twofer*!" says Veronica, handing us our badges. "Two badges in one challenge. I've never seen that before. You keep surprising me, Moxie."

I'm not sure which is glowing brighter, my heart or the pile of burning twigs at my feet.

Next, Veronica shows us how to cook the trout, which we eat with bread and beans.

"As I promised, tonight we'll have an Iron Gut challenge—a chance to touch and taste and eat something *truly unusual*."

There is a ripple of excitement. Opportunities for an Iron Gut challenge are rare. Everyone is chattering about what this one might be.

Once it was a chocolate-covered grasshopper.

Once it was the stomach of a cow.

And tonight's challenge is . . . . trout eyeballs.

There is an "*OOOhhhhh*" and an "*UGGGhhhh*," and then a bunch of boasting.

"Who is going to try?"

Of course, the Dublingers will not try. They got their Iron Gut badges ages ago.

"I will," says Hilly, who already has hers, too, but apparently enjoys punishing her stomach. "How about you, Moxie?" she asks with a wink.

Of course, I never would and never will eat the eyeball of a fish.

Nope, I say.

No way, and no thank you. Not for a badge or twenty badges. Not for twenty dollars.

"Oh, *come* on," Hilly pleads, plucking an eyeball from the plate Veronica is holding.

"Give it a try, Moxie," says Veronica, and something about the way she is smiling makes it actually impossible not to grab a tiny eyeball and place it on my plate, where it will sit until the end of time, uneaten and unloved.

Hilly pops an eyeball into her mouth and gives a few chews.

"What does it taste like?"

"Not much. Just kind of like chewing on rubber. No big deal!"

"I'm glad you like it!" says Veronica. "Perhaps we need to make a *Super* Iron Gut badge for our true pioneers."

I bristle at the praise I am not getting, but I have my standards, and I intend to stick to them.

We sit there for a while,
eating our meal and watching
the fire as the sky grows black.

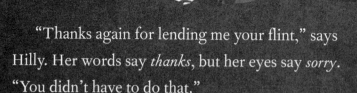

"Thanks again for lending me your flint," says Hilly. Her words say *thanks*, but her eyes say *sorry*. "You didn't have to do that."

I think about it for a moment, but she's not quite right. We were out of balance, and I needed to set things right. "Actually, I think I *did*."

"Well, we're even now," she says with a smile.

My body sighs in pure relief. Now that Hilly and I are friends again, my appetite returns with a fury. Knowing that I am eating a trout *I caught by myself* and cooked over a fire *I started by myself* makes my dinner taste all the more delicious.

Moxie.

Hilly has a look on her face. I motion that I am right in the middle of a bite and that I will answer her as soon as I'm done.

Moxie!

I finish chewing and carefully swallow, wanting to make it very clear for everyone present that I will not be rushed and prefer not to talk with my mouth full.

Now . . .

what is it?

Hilly gives me a pitying sort of look. "You just ate the eyeball."

"Excuse me?" Because it sounds like Hilly said I just ate the eyeball, which, as I made perfectly clear, I would *never* do.

Hilly points to the part of my plate where the eyeball was. It is notably gone.

"What the—?!"

"You scooped it up with your last bite of

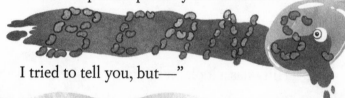

I tried to tell you, but—"

I'm trying to figure out the fastest way to turn the contents of my stomach inside out when Veronica walks over and hands me the

IRON GUT

badge. And the combination of her proud look and Tracy Dublinger's somewhat worried face makes me decide that perhaps the eyeball should stay where it is after all.

We roast s'mores. We sing campfire songs. Which gives me an idea.

"If a Wonder Scout were to write her own song and sing it for the other Scouts, could it count for the Artist badge?"

Veronica makes a thinking face. "I guess it would depend on the song. Have you written one?"

"Well, not *just* me," I say, glancing over at Hilly. "Should we—?"

Hilly's eyes light up. I don't have to finish my sentence. She knows exactly what I'm asking.

We stand a few paces apart, facing each other.

Uno, dos, tres,

I sing, shuffling to the right.

Cuatro, cinco, seis,

Hilly responds, sliding to the left.

Siete!

I kick my right leg high.

Ocho!

She kicks her left leg even higher.

Nueve!

I shake my booty.

Diez!

Hilly shakes her booty, too.

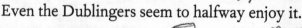

We plow through the other languages, each with its own set of dance moves. By the time we finish, we're laughing so hard we fall down. And so is everyone else. The Scouts *Cheer.* Even the Dublingers seem to halfway enjoy it.

"Another twofer! Amazing!" says Veronica, handing Hilly the Artist and the Polyglot badges, and the Artist badge to me.

"I'd like to challenge for my Polyglot," says Megan Lacy, perhaps inspired by our song.

"Me too," says Henrietta, suddenly more animated than I've ever seen her before.

"I'm glad you're all so excited about what you're learning," says Veronica. "But I think we're done for tonight. How about we have some additional badge challenges at Monday's meeting?"

We cheer in agreement that this sounds like a very good plan.

"Tell us a story!" Hilly begs.

"It's getting pretty late," says Veronica.

"It's *early*!" I insist.

"*Tell* us," pleads Henrietta.

"Tell us how you got your compass," says Hilly. "It's my favorite story," she whispers to me.

"All right," says Veronica, smiling. "Just one story. And then to bed!"

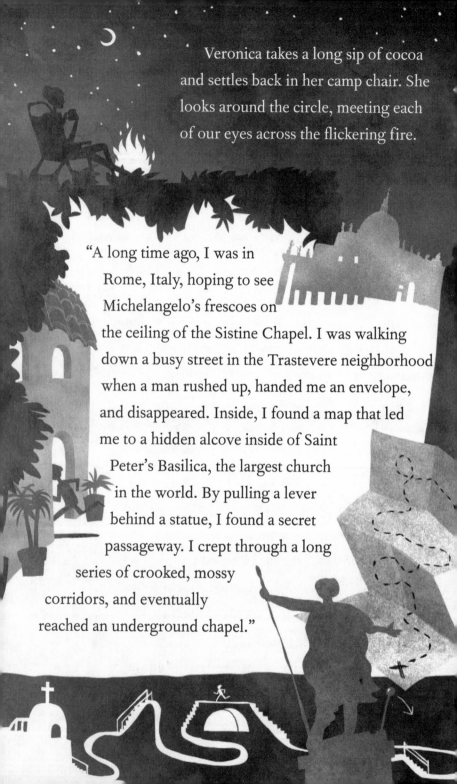

Veronica takes a long sip of cocoa and settles back in her camp chair. She looks around the circle, meeting each of our eyes across the flickering fire.

"A long time ago, I was in Rome, Italy, hoping to see Michelangelo's frescoes on the ceiling of the Sistine Chapel. I was walking down a busy street in the Trastevere neighborhood when a man rushed up, handed me an envelope, and disappeared. Inside, I found a map that led me to a hidden alcove inside of Saint Peter's Basilica, the largest church in the world. By pulling a lever behind a statue, I found a secret passageway. I crept through a long series of crooked, mossy corridors, and eventually reached an underground chapel."

"How did you see?" I have to know.

A high-powered flashlight. A Wonder Scout is always prepared.

I find myself marveling all over again as Veronica continues. "A one-hundred-twenty-seven-year-old monk was standing in the shadows. He said he'd been waiting for me for eighty years."

"Eighty years?" It seems impossible.

"He said he had been *expecting* me."

"But you weren't even born when he started waiting!"

"That's what makes it so amazing!" says Hilly. "Tell us what happened next!"

"He asked me to answer a riddle."

"What was it?!"

Veronica pauses as we all lean toward her.

What's worth more than gold and costs less than dust?

Hilly is so excited she can hardly contain herself. Everyone is looking at everyone else, trying not to burst. I realize I'm the only one who doesn't know the answer.

Well, Moxie?

says Veronica.

I think and think. I'm pretty sure

PLATINUM *IS WORTH MORE THAN* **GOLD**

but it's definitely on the pricey side. I try to think of anything that costs less than dust, which, the last time I checked, is entirely free.

And so I am forced to say three of my least favorite words.

I don't know.

Veronica smiles her smile of endless wisdom.

EXPERIENCE.

And my brain kicks itself for not thinking of it.

"That's from the Credo!" says Henrietta.

Suddenly, I remember:

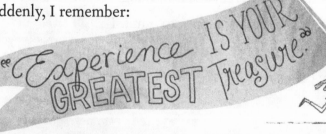

"Experience IS YOUR GREATEST Treasure."

"Yes," says Veronica. "Without *experience*, you can't grow. You can't learn from your mistakes. You can't build on your discoveries. But you get experience every moment of your life, for free, wherever you go, whether you want it or not. Each and every one of you is a great big pile of experience that gets taller and mightier every minute."

I imagine my pile. It is extremely impressive.

"So . . . what happened next?" asks Hilly, who knows the answer but wants to hear it anyway.

"The monk smiled and handed me a little

The wood was so old, it started to crumble when I lifted the lid. Inside, on a tiny golden pedestal, I found this."

Veronica holds up her compass for all of us to see. It glitters fantastically in the light of the campfire. It is ancient and beautiful.

"The old man told me I had a strong inner compass that would lead me exactly where I needed to go. And he told me to always remember that I am capable of astonishing things."

"That's from the Credo, too!" says Henrietta.

Veronica smiles. "At that moment, I knew that I had to keep adventuring and that I had to pass the old man's wisdom along to other girls."

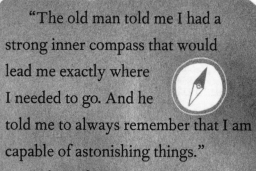

Then what happened?

Hilly can't stand even the slightest pause.

The old monk told me it was time for me to go . . . . because he needed to take a nap.

A nap?

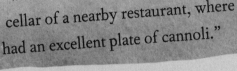

"He was extremely tired. He showed me a door to another tunnel, which led to a hidden door in the wine cellar of a nearby restaurant, where I had an excellent plate of cannoli."

"What's that?"

"A crunchy Italian pastry stuffed with a sweet, creamy filling!" says Hilly. "Did you bring us some, Veronica?"

"As a matter of fact, I just whipped up a fresh batch this afternoon," says Veronica, pulling out a container with twelve little pastries inside.

As we munch our cannoli,

my mind does cannonballs into

A SWIMMING POOL of delight.

Once again, Veronica's story is as amazing as anything I've read in Annabelle Adams.

"Time for bed," says Veronica. All of us groan our disappointment. We never want this night to end.

By the time we crawl into our sleeping bags, it's so dark I could be floating in the distant void of outer space. So dark I don't know for sure whether I still have legs and arms and hands. I would turn on my flashlight, but I can't find my flashlight. And I can't find Homer. The only sensation is the pulsing of crickets. It's so dark that I don't even know if I'm alive.

Hilly?

Yeah?

My heart flutters with relief just knowing she's there.

Nothing.

What is it?

Nothing.

Okay.

But I need something more than hearing her
voice in the dark. I need to know she's actually
there. I need to know for *sure*.

And so I say two words I've never said out loud.

I'm scared.

I brace for laughter or a snort or a scoff that says fourth
graders aren't supposed to be afraid of the dark.

But Hilly says nothing at all. She reaches over and finds
my hand and gives it a squeeze.

And instead of letting go, she holds on. Eventually, the
squeeze lets up and her breathing gets slower
as she drifts off to sleep.

A minute later, I am riding
an iridescent eagle
through a butter-moon sky.

I wake when the sun comes up.

There is Homer, right where he's supposed to be.

Hilly is still asleep, so I crawl out of the tent and help

Veronica start the fire and mix some batter and

make pancakes. The morning is crisp and

clear. I'm the only Scout awake so far.

"That was quite a performance last night," says Veronica. "Something tells me you might have done a little practice."

I glow like a radioactive frog that just climbed out of a vat of and is getting ready to turn into a superhero.

"I'm *very* glad you've joined us, Moxie."

"I'm *very* glad you traveled the world learning remarkable things."

"You're the reason I did it."

"Me?"

"You and the rest of the Scouts."

"Ankthay ouyay!"

"On'tday etlay osethay ancakespay urnbay," says Veronica, nodding at the pancakes, which are in fact starting to get a little crispy.

One by one, the other Scouts emerge with their morning hair and faces, slightly rumpled and not quite entirely awake. As we eat breakfast, Henrietta is a little less nervous. The Dublingers are a little less mean. All of us are maybe just a little bit more like ourselves.

249

CHAPTER 14: MILTON'S TEST KITCHEN

On the way home from Boo Mountain, Hilly and I hatch a plan to make a good weekend even better.

Dad calls Hilly's parents, who say Okay,

and Emily's dads, who say No problem,

and so we pick Emily up on the way back home.

At some point in a long afternoon spent laughing and talking and having the kind of fun you can only have on a sleepover with your two best friends, I realize I've never had two best friends at the same time in my whole entire life.

In the morning, I make pancakes.

I am not usually much help in the kitchen, and Dad seems worried that I might burn down the house, but I tell him he doesn't need to worry, because

GIRLS CAN DO ANYTHING.

He cooks some bacon to go with the pancakes, and then he goes out to do dad things in the yard, leaving Emily, Hilly, and me to enjoy our perfect day.

That's when Milton walks in wearing his tool belt and a chef's hat from the costume box.

Enough speculation!

he says, holding his tiny finger in the air.

To defeat a Dublinger, we must think like a Dublinger. We must do what a Dublinger does.

I like where this is going.

Please continue,

I say.

251

"Hilly, would you be willing to walk me through the meringue-making process?" Milton asks.

"Sure," says Hilly. "Moxie, would you get everything ready?"

I get out the

, the  and the

"First, make sure your bowl is clean and dry," says Hilly. "Meringue is very fussy."

Milton carefully washes and dries the bowl.

"Next, separate the

 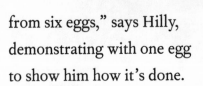

from six eggs," says Hilly, demonstrating with one egg to show him how it's done.

Milton replicates the technique perfectly on his first try. Of course.

Be extra careful not to get *any* yolk in the whites,

says Hilly.

Why is that?

Milton is suddenly quite interested.

The fats in the yolk keep the proteins in the whites from sticking together,

she says.

So you can't mix *any* yolk in with the whites, or the meringue won't rise.

Maybe *that* is what's causing problems for Tammy!

Emily suggests.

But I've watched, and Tammy is *incredibly* careful,

I say.

She never gets even a speck of yolk in her bowl.

Milton is deep in egg-related thought.

Next, we add one-quarter of a teaspoon of cream of tartar to stabilize the meringue,

says Hilly.

"And then we're ready to turn on the mixer?" asks Milton, who is a sucker for machines of any kind and loves nothing more than turning them on.

Yes, but . . .

Whatever Hilly was going to say next is lost as Milton flips the SWITCH and all of us are instantly bespattered with frantically flung egg whites.

". . . be sure *not* to turn it on while the speed is set on high," says Hilly, turning off the mixer and wiping egg from her face.

"Here," she says, adjusting the speed and turning on the mixer again. Milton barely registers the mess. His brain is focused on the bigger picture. As is mine.

254

"If there's nothing wrong with Tammy's eggs . . ." I say.

"And she definitely doesn't mix any yolks in with her whites . . ." says Milton.

"Then the only possible explanation is . . ." I say.

Milton and I lock eyes as he continues, " . . . that Tracy is . . ."

We share a knowing nod. At the very same moment, we have figured it out.

What? says Hilly.

Tell us! Emily insists.

And so we do.

"Dastardly," says Emily.

"Delightful," says Hilly, testing the consistency of the meringue, which has turned out just fine, even though there's far less of it than we'd originally planned.

"Not quite as delightful as solving a mystery," I say.

"And not nearly as scrumptious as solving *two*," says Hilly.

"What about the *other* Dublinger?" asks Hilly.

Milton takes off his chef's hat and puts on his jacket. "I was hoping you'd say that," he says. "Grab your map and compass and come with me."

We walk to the Commons.

"Show me how orienteering works," says Milton.

Hilly shows Milton how to use the map and compass to determine where he is and to navigate to specific coordinates. He picks up the concept quickly, but he's having zero luck finding the right spot in the park.

"Maybe you're reading the map wrong," I say, leaning over.

I see from the look on Milton's face that an idea is taking root in that great big brain. He removes the Magnetron 2000 from his tool belt and hands it to me.

"Moxie, don't take this personally, but could you please go stand by that distant bench for a minute?"

"Please tell me how I could not take that personally."

It might help us catch a Dublinger,

he says with a grin.

I reluctantly oblige. I would eat a burrito full of bumblebees in order to catch a Dublinger.

Milton tries again, and this time he navigates easily to the red oak tree.

"Perfect!" says Hilly.

"Milton should definitely join Wonder Scouts," says Emily.

Milton is soaring like the blimp above a football game.

Our work here is done,

he says.

As I hand the Magnetron 2000 back to Milton, I suddenly realize what Tammy has been doing to dupe Tracy. I'm not quite sure *how* she is doing it, but that should be easy enough to figure out.

"Simply diabolical," I say, holding up my hand to give Milton a high five. And by taking a bit of a running start and making a mighty leap, he manages to plant his palm flat against mine in a way that is both satisfying and loud.

Once again, Hilly and Emily go wild, demanding explanations. I marvel at the

EVIL GENIUS

of the Dublingers and the

BRILLIANT FORCE for GOOD

that is my little brother.

When we get back to the house, Milton goes to his room to pore over his collection of Local House of History newspaper clippings, and Hilly and I get down to the business of persuading Emily to join Wonder Scouts despite the potential medical implications.

Milton is amazing, says Emily.

He truly is, I say,

but do you want to hear something even *more* amazing?

Sure!

I glance at Hilly.

Tell Emily the story of Veronica's compass.

But that's . . . a Wonder Scout secret, says Hilly with a worried look.

I give Hilly a look of my own. She's messing with the plan. "But if Emily is going to join . . . we'd just be giving her a *sneak preview* of the stories she'll hear eventually, right?"

"Are you really going to join?" asks Hilly.

"I *think* so," says Emily. "I'd *like* to."

Hilly spends a few more seconds looking worried, but then she gives in and tells it all.

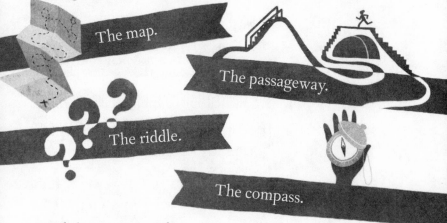

The map.

The passageway.

The riddle.

The compass.

Emily's eyes are wide.

"Isn't that incredible?" asks Hilly when she's done.

But Emily looks sort of green, which happens sometimes. As much as I love her, she isn't very sturdy.

"I'm sorry, but . . . I have to go."

"What's wrong?"

"I'm not feeling well."

Amazing! Even just thinking about becoming a Wonder Scout is giving Emily

"I'll ask Dad to drive you home."

Hilly and I help Emily gather her stuff, and we wish her good-bye. On the way out the door, Emily says something to Milton, who shakes his head.

What did she ask you?

I ask Milton when Emily is gone.

She wanted to know if I had any new clues relating to the Local House of History case.

Weird,

I say.

But Milton says nothing. He tugs on his earlobe and watches as Emily follows Dad out to our car.

For the rest of the afternoon, Hilly and I have the kind of fun that you can only have with one best friend. Which, it turns out, is still pretty great.

But even the greatest weekend in the history of weekends has to end eventually. I lie in bed, remembering it fondly, and start thinking ahead to the next one.

Suddenly, I have everything I need to solve Tammy's case . . . and to turn the tables and expose her own thoroughly unsisterly crime.

CHAPTER 15: TWO THEORIES

Look at this, says Milton at breakfast on Monday, pointing to a story in the *Tiddlywhump Times*. The headline on his face makes clear that the news is big.

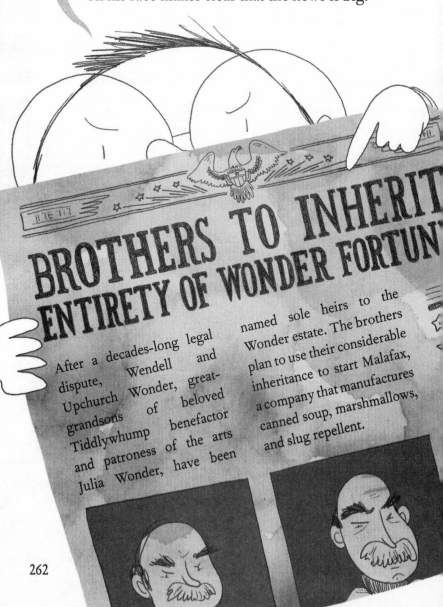

BROTHERS TO INHERIT ENTIRETY OF WONDER FORTUN

After a decades-long legal dispute, Wendell and Upchurch Wonder, great-grandsons of beloved Tiddlywhump benefactor and patroness of the arts Julia Wonder, have been named sole heirs to the Wonder estate. The brothers plan to use their considerable inheritance to start Malafax, a company that manufactures canned soup, marshmallows, and slug repellent.

I gasp for a full **7** seconds.

For the first time in my life, I have encountered something more loathsome than a Dublinger.

Milton gets right to the point. "*Sole* heirs?"

"But isn't Veronica their cousin?"

"According to the family tree, yes."

"Then why wouldn't she *also* be an heir?"

Milton nods grimly, his face **an ocean of concern.**

My brain is working overtime to make sense of it all.

Maybe . . . the folder contained a **Legal Document** that was Veronica's only way of proving that *she* is also a rightful heir to the family fortune, *and so her cousins stole it!*

Milton gives me a look that says, *Don't stop now—you're really on a roll.*

And maybe . . .

My brain grabs all the loose threads we've been gathering over the past few weeks and tries to knit them into one beautiful rope.

Maybe . . . the Chief Historian caught Wendell and Upchurch in the act, but then they bribed him into letting them escape by saying they'd cut him in on the inheritance!

Milton's eyes grow wide. This mystery has the opportunity to rival the Case of the Missing Lunch Box.

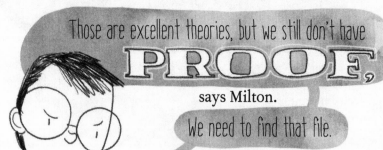

Those are excellent theories, but we still don't have **PROOF,** says Milton.

We need to find that file.

"Where do Wendell and Upchurch live?" I am considering a stakeout.

Milton reads the article again.

he says drearily.

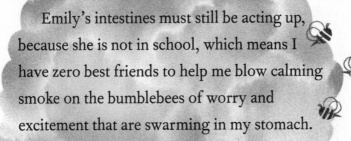

I suddenly stop considering a stakeout.

We sit there in silence, eating our breakfast and feeling flattened by the weight of things we do not know.

Emily's intestines must still be acting up, because she is not in school, which means I have zero best friends to help me blow calming smoke on the bumblebees of worry and excitement that are swarming in my stomach.

I'm sure Mr. Shine can tell I'm not exactly listening as he talks about symbiosis, whatever that is. All I know is that I need Emily and she needs me, like two independent organisms that mutually benefit from spending time together.

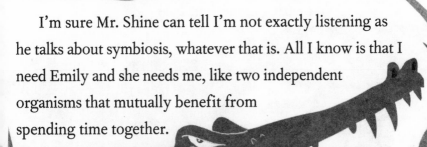

All day long, I practice for tonight's meeting. Exactly what I'll say. Exactly what I'll do. The part of me that wants to pay attention to Mr. Shine is being sat on by the part of me that has to figure out how to fly blindfolded on a hang glider through a narrow canyon filled with booby traps and angry vultures.

I take out a sheet of paper and write Tammy a note.

I've figured out how Tracy is messing you up. Let me challenge first tonight, and I'll explain everything.

—MM

On our walk home from school, Milton is wearing his serious face.

Maybe we can't get our hands on that folder, he says.

But we have to tell Veronica what we know. And what we suspect.

Milton is right. Veronica has a right to know that her cousins are *conspiring* against her.

"I wouldn't want to have that conversation in front of the other Scouts, but Veronica comes to meetings directly from work. Maybe we could talk to her there," I suggest.

"Let's see if Dad can take us to the

Library on the way to the community center tonight."

Milton's face makes it clear there's something he's not saying.

"There's something you're not saying."

"I have a thought that's not quite ready to come out."

And as much as I want to know what it is, I know better than to push.

We ask, and Dad says, "Sure." And why would he not? What dad doesn't want his kids to spend time at the library?

First, we have dinner, which is **TACOS.**

Nothing goes better with tacos than **ROOT BEER.**

"Could we please have some root beer with dinner tonight?" I ask, batting my eyes while wondering why this is something a person is supposed to do when that person wants something.

"What's the occasion?" asks Dad. We only have soda on very special occasions.

"I plan to do something rather remarkable this evening."

Dad smiles. "Do I get to hear what it is?"

"Afterward," I say. "For now, it's a **SURPRISE.**

"Well then," says Dad, pulling out the root beer and pouring us each a big glass. Apparently, the eye batting worked.

Cheers! he says.

Cheers, says Milton.

Cheers, I say, as convincingly as I can. But I am too focused for actual cheer.

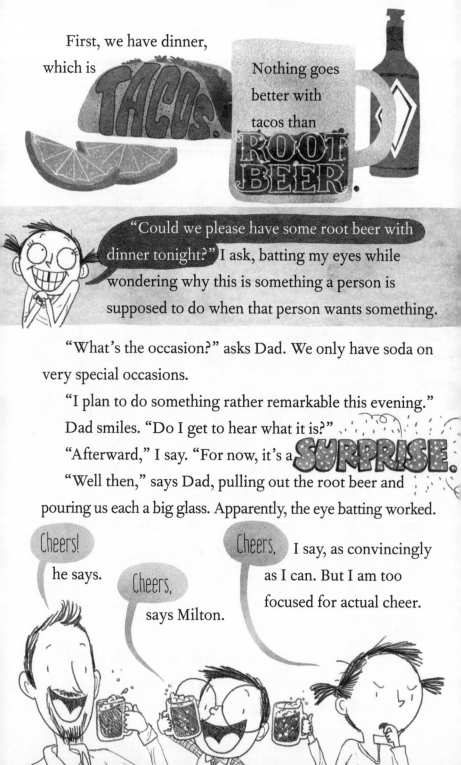

When we finish dinner, I grab

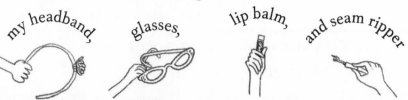

my headband, glasses, lip balm, and seam ripper

and head for the car. It's time to go, but Milton is nowhere to
be found.

I find him on the other side of the bathroom door.

Hurry up! I say.

I'm going as
fast as I can!

he insists.

Dad takes us to the library.

"We won't be long," I say.

"No problem," says Dad, who always enjoys having a
few free minutes to play Lollipop Obliterator on his phone.

We get out of the car, and I scurry toward the door. But
Milton is limping along like his leg is about to fall off.

"Hurry up!"

"My leg fell asleep in the car!"

I look at my watch. The meeting
starts in 15 minutes.

I practically drag Milton up the front steps.

We go to the circulation desk and ask for Veronica.

"I think she's in her office," says the head librarian, Mrs. Wilhelmina Smithers. She could give the Chief Historian a run for his money in the personality game.

When we get to Veronica's office, the light is off. I look out the window into the back parking lot and see her getting into her car.

UGH!

I say, trying not to show how angry I am with Milton.

If we hurry, we might be able to catch her before she drives away.

But Milton is not there.

"Where did you *go?*" I ask, completely out of patience. Milton does not reply, but I hear the telltale sound of someone riffling through someone else's filing cabinet.

What are you *doing*?

I am shocked and scandalized.

Indulging a hunch.

Stop looking at Veronica's private things! That's not okay!

No . . . *this* is not okay!

says Milton, holding up a folder marked with the LOCAL HOUSE HISTORY seal.

Is that . . . ?

I can hardly get the words out.

But why would Veronica . . . steal her *own* folder?

That's the question I intend to answer.

I'm sure there's a simple explanation. Put it back.

If there's nothing to hide, why don't we take a look?

Mrs. Smithers pokes her head in. "Why are you two standing in the dark?" she asks in a way that is neither patient nor polite.

Milton quickly stuffs the 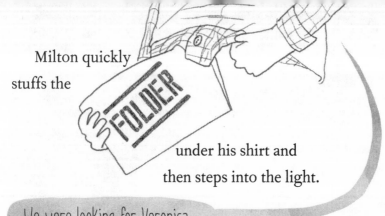 under his shirt and then steps into the light.

We were looking for Veronica, he says.

It seems clear she isn't here.

We're almost done, I say.

We just need a moment to put the folder back.

You're done *now*, she says.

I will walk you out.

It is not a suggestion.

As we scamper back to the car, my heart sinks as I try to imagine how the file could have found its way into Veronica's drawer.

We get to the community center a minute before the meeting begins.

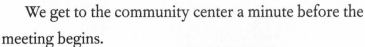Good luck tonight,

says Dad.

"Thanks," I say.

As I step out of the car, I give Milton a look. "I hope things go well with your . . . research project."

Milton looks appropriately grim.

I'll let you know what I learn.

CHAPTER 16: INTO THE DARK

The meeting begins. We sing the song. We say the Credo. As I requested, Tammy seems content to sit back and let me take the lead, but before Veronica can even ask, Tracy blurts,

I CHALLENGE!! ORIENTEER!

Before Veronica can respond, I cut in.

Excuse me, but haven't Tammy and Tracy gone first in the last two badge challenges? Wouldn't it be fair to let someone *not* named Dublinger go first tonight?

I get the double-dark glare I expected.

"Yes, that does seem fair," says Veronica. "And I'm assuming *you* would like to go first?"

"Yes . . . if you don't mind . . . I would like to challenge for the Scientist badge."

"How exciting," says Veronica. "What hypothesis are you hoping to test?"

"If you don't mind, I'd like to demonstrate while I tell you."

Veronica gives me a dignified nod that lets me know she doesn't mind at all.

Everyone here knows the recipe for making meringue.

I gather the mixing bowl and ingredients as I talk.

Yet some of us have struggled despite having all the necessary skills.

Tammy eyes me suspiciously.

AS SHE SHOULD.

I've been wondering what could keep a person with the incredible focus and technique of Tammy Dublinger from making perfect meringue every time she tried.

Anyone?

Twelve sets of earlobes are hanging on my every word.

SCIENCE!

I say, lifting my arm majestically.

"Science?" asks Veronica.

YES! I say. Suppose I were to put something greasy into this bowl. . . .

I take out my tub of lip balm, dig my finger in, and smear a **GREAT, GREASY BLOB** on the inside of the bowl.

"What are you *doing*?" shouts Tracy, outraged. Next to her, Tammy smolders like an angry ember.

"Science!" I say, cracking and separating six eggs with the grace and conviction of an Olympic figure skater spinning effortlessly at the end of her routine.

I add the cream of tartar and turn on the mixer.
But meringue does not occur.

"As you can see, this gloopy disaster looks
pretty much like Tammy's recent efforts."

"HEY!" says Tammy.

"It's not your fault," I say, to calm
Tammy down before I lose an arm. "Any
chemist would say that you have been
thwarted by . . . *science*! However, if you
repeat the same experiment with
a *clean* bowl . . ."

I pull out the extra bowl I have brought
from the kitchen for this very purpose.

With the mechanical precision of a robot
designed specifically to do jujitsu ballet, I crack six
more eggs and mix up a meringue so stiff and fluffy
and tall that even Annabelle would be proud.

There is a collective

from all but one of the Scouts.

As it turns out, it is scientifically *impossible* for egg whites to stiffen in the presence of a greasy substance! I'm guessing that Tammy's bowl must not have been entirely clean.

I ALWAYS CLEAN MY BOWL!

says Tammy, outraged.

"Then perhaps it's possible that something greasy was *deliberately* placed in your bowl *after* you cleaned it? Though I can't *imagine* how that could have happened."

As my fellow Wonder Scouts applaud, I allow myself the briefest glimpse at Tammy, who is glaring at Tracy like a panther that's ready for lunch.

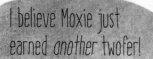

I believe Moxie just earned *another* twofer!

says Veronica, reaching into her pouch and handing me two badges.

SCIENTIST AND MASTER BAKER.

Well done! Now, would anyone else like to—

"If you don't mind," I interrupt as politely as I can, "my demonstration is not *quite* complete. I would like to share a related *mystery* with my fellow Scouts."

"But now I want to challenge for the Master Baker!" says Tammy, like the hare that finally figured out how the tortoise keeps winning, and just wants to finish the race.

"I'm sorry, but Moxie just used up all the eggs," says Veronica, clearly irritated by Tammy's interruption. "Moxie, why don't you tell us about your *mystery*?"

"I have noticed that Tracy Dublinger has been unable to earn her Orienteering badge, and I have been trying to figure out why. After all, she knows how to read a map. She knows how to use a compass. She has the competitive drive of a Thoroughbred racehorse. And the killer instinct of a ravenous jackal. And the glistening white teeth of a well-groomed walrus. And the—"

"Where are you going with this, Moxie?" asks Veronica.

"My point is that it doesn't make a lot of sense that Tracy wouldn't have earned her Orienteering badge by now unless . . ."

"Unless?" says Veronica.

"Unless?" say Tracy and Tammy at the same time.

"Unless . . . there has been . . . FOUL PLAY!" I say, widening my eyes to show just how foul the play has been.

Foul play?

Veronica asks.

Foul play?

Tammy sneers, glaring at me with fury.

Foul play?

Tracy hisses, glaring at Tammy
with fury times two.

Even the most determined Scout won't have much luck following her map if, instead of pointing north, the needle points to . . .

To what?

asks Veronica.

To what?

demands Tracy.

To what?

says Tammy, with the look of someone
who just ate the eyeball of a trout.

281

I pull out my compass and walk over to Tracy, who holds up her hands as if she thinks I might whack her with it. But as much as I might like to, I have a different plan.

"Do not worry, Tracy," I say. "This isn't going to hurt a bit."

Starting at the upper corner of her sash, I move the compass diagonally down the row of badges. And, just as I suspected, instead of pointing north, the needle points to . . .

Tracy's **LEFT KIDNEY.**

With apologies, I say as I take out my seam ripper and remove Tracy's Polyglot badge in two swift strokes.

HEY! Tracy snarls.

EUREKA! I say, holding up the small but powerful magnet that was sewn in behind Tracy's badge.

Mystery solved!

RAITOR!

shrieks Tracy, lunging toward Tammy the way a famished hippopotamus might lunge at a clump of particularly delectable grass.

With instincts that rival those of a well-rested ninja, I grab the potted plant and halfway lift it halfway slide it and halfway throw it into the rapidly closing space between Tammy and Tracy.

Rather than bothering to run *around* the plant, Tracy attempts to jump *over* it, which goes badly for Tracy.

And even worse for the plant.

By the time Tracy gets herself untangled, all the fight seems to have left her.

"I wonder if that was the kind of strength that would qualify for the Mighty badge?" I say to no one in particular.

"Nice try," says Veronica. "But even *that* is not the kind of strength the Mighty badge is all about. Are you finished with your demonstration?" she asks in the astonished sort of voice one might use when poking one's head out of a cyclone shelter after a tornado has passed.

Not quite,

I say, placing my hands on my hips, leaning back a little, and letting out the loudest, longest, most confident, and ROOT-BEER-SMELLING-EST BELCH in the history of belches. The only way in which it falls short of the least ladylike belch of all time is that it does not ring the Wonder Bell.

"What do we think, Scouts? Does Moxie's belch qualify for—?" But Veronica doesn't even finish her sentence before a collective

YES!!!"

fills the room.

"If you will excuse me for a moment," I say. "The last part of the demonstration is proving that Tracy's map and compass work just fine. Is the cache in the same place it was last time?"

"Yes."

"In that case, I'll be back in a jiffy."

Before Tracy can realize what's happening, I grab her

and race out the back door.

I plunge into the night. It is very dark, and I suddenly realize that this is a *terrible* idea. But then I remember Milton's

TINY BUT VERY BRIGHT

FLASHLIGHT

which he lent to me to use in this precise moment. *A Wonder Scout is always prepared*, I say to myself.

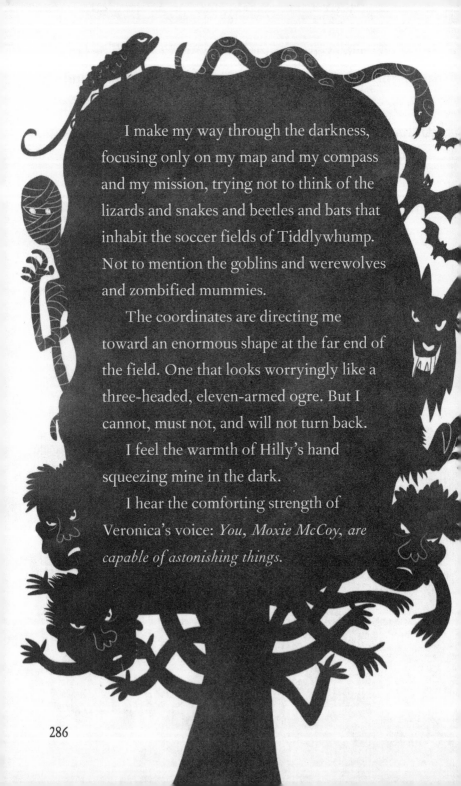

I make my way through the darkness, focusing only on my map and my compass and my mission, trying not to think of the lizards and snakes and beetles and bats that inhabit the soccer fields of Tiddlywhump. Not to mention the goblins and werewolves and zombified mummies.

The coordinates are directing me toward an enormous shape at the far end of the field. One that looks worryingly like a three-headed, eleven-armed ogre. But I cannot, must not, and will not turn back.

I feel the warmth of Hilly's hand squeezing mine in the dark.

I hear the comforting strength of Veronica's voice: *You, Moxie McCoy, are capable of astonishing things.*

But there in the darkness, the words make no sense, so I say them out loud.

I, Moxie McCoy, am capable of astonishing things!

It helps a little, so I say it again.

And again.

And again.

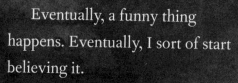

Eventually, a funny thing happens. Eventually, I sort of start believing it.

I shine my flashlight on the enormous shape. It is not even a one-headed, two-armed ogre. It is an eastern cottonwood. And there, in the crook at the base of the trunk, is a little metal box that contains the Orienteering badge.

I race back across the field on lightning feet, certain that I am being chased by seven hungry goblin kings. My moment of bravery seems to have expired.

But then I see warm light shining through the community center windows, and my heart lifts. A moment later, I am back inside, triumphantly holding up the badge.

Moxie earns the Orienteering badge! And the Detective badge! And the Loudest Belch!

"So . . . is that a *three*fer?" asks Hilly.

"It is!" says Veronica. *"Amazing!"*

Everyone is cheering except Tammy, who continues to sulk about the lack of eggs, and Tracy, who is demanding to challenge for the Orienteering badge herself, only to learn from Veronica that she can try again on Wednesday, once a new cache has been hidden.

I stand there, surrounded by my fellow Scouts, feeling an excitement that's bigger than myself. It's a moment so perfect that nothing can possibly ruin it.

Which is why it's so upsetting when I hear Veronica say, "Hello. Can I help you?"

Followed by Henrietta Bork saying, "Doesn't that boy look kind of like that pizza guy?"

I turn, and there is Milton with a look that means nothing but trouble.

CHAPTER 17: WHEN IN ROME

Excuse me, but can you spare Moxie for a minute?

Of course,

says Veronica, wrinkling up her nose with amusement.

As I follow Milton into the lobby, my fellow Scouts begin a game of Simon Says.

What is it? I hiss.

I'm in the middle of something.

We wouldn't have come if it weren't so important.

We?

Emily steps out from behind a potted plant with the look of someone who has just been bitten by an otter she had mistakenly assumed was friendly.

What is it, you guys? What's going on?

"I read through Veronica's file," says Milton. Something is wrong, but I don't want to hear it. "I'm going back to the meeting."

"Take a look, Moxie," says Emily with eyes full of sorrow and love. *"Please."*

I take the folder. I open it up. Inside is a clipping from the newspaper of a little town about 100 miles from Tiddlywhump.

The Johnsonville Herald

LOCAL HERO MOVING ON

The citizens of Johnsonville thank Ronnie Collins, the great-granddaughter of renowned philanthropist and arts patroness Julia Wonder, for ten years of faithful service to our library. We wish her the best of luck on her next adventure.

But this article is from two years ago. Which means . . .

As I suddenly realize the awful truth, my brain fights hard to come up with another explanation.

291

But Milton speaks the thought I can't bring myself to put into words.

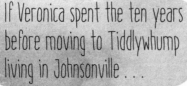

If Veronica spent the ten years before moving to Tiddlywhump living in Johnsonville . . .

He wants me to be the one to

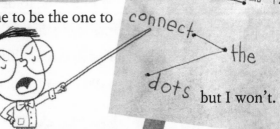

connect the dots but I won't.

. . . she couldn't have traveled the world taming tiger cubs, exploring lost ruins, and finding sacred artifacts,

says Emily.

There must be a simple explanation.

"Maybe she did her adventuring during holidays?" I suggest.

Emily pulls out a book.

"What's that?"

Constance Cavendish
VOLUME 13
When in Rome.

What about it?

Page one hundred thirty-four,

she says, handing the book to me.

I turn to page 134 and read about a feisty teenager named Constance Cavendish who receives a . . .

secret map that leads her to a hidden passageway inside . . . Saint Peter's Basilica, where she meets a . . . 127-year-old monk who makes her solve a riddle and gives her . . . an enchanted compass. The riddle is different, but pretty much everything else is the same.

My heart shrivels into a small, heavy stone.

Emily puts her hand on my shoulder. "Constance Cavendish is a British series about a young librarian who loves to read and uses her vast knowledge to solve puzzles and fight injustice. I read a few of the books when my dads and I were in London last year, and I recognized the compass story."

293

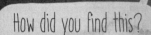How did you find this?

I ask, holding up the 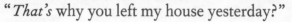, which suddenly feels like the anchor of an ocean liner.

"I looked online and found it at the Johnsonville library. My dads drove me over there yesterday afternoon, and I checked out the entire series."

"*That's* why you left my house yesterday?"

"Yeah."

"And . . . did you share your suspicions with Milton on your way out the door?"

"I did."

"That's what made me think we might find the folder in Veronica's office," says Milton.

"Which is why you *stalled* on our way to the library . . . so that Veronica would already be gone when we got there!" I say, remembering Milton's *I have to go to the bathroom* and *My leg fell asleep in the car* routine.

Milton doesn't deny it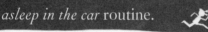

"Why did you guys keep me in the dark?"

"We know how you feel about Veronica," says Emily. "We didn't want to upset you unless we could find actual proof."

My brain is stuck between EXTREMELY ANGRY & INCREDIBLY TOUCHED.

I have a truly awful thought. "Did you miss school today so that you could read through the entire Constance Cavendish series until you found this page?"

"I did."

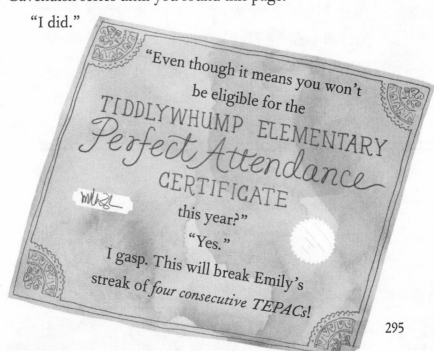

"Even though it means you won't be eligible for the

TIDDLYWHUMP ELEMENTARY
Perfect Attendance
CERTIFICATE

this year?"

"Yes."

I gasp. This will break Emily's streak of *four* consecutive TEPACs!

"And did you *just now* find the passage and ask your dad or your other dad—I'm sorry that I can't ever remember their names—to drive you over here in the *middle of the meeting* so that you could deliver this devastating but important news at the *soonest possible moment*?"

Emily nods, her  full of

I couldn't stand to see you getting fooled for even one more minute.

My heart has been defeated, so my epic brain takes over.

No. This is all just a *coincidence*.

There's something *else* in the file, says Milton, lifting up the clipping and revealing a letter.

Dear Veronica,

You are a baby, and I am an old woman. I will likely be gone before I can teach you the wisdom I have gained. And so I am writing down my best advice. I learned each of these lessons the hard way. With any luck, you can use them to be a better and wiser woman than I am.

1. You don't need to be proper or quiet or sweet. You need to be you.
2. But never be mean. Especially to other girls.
3. Do not aspire to be normal. It is the opposite of interesting.
4. Never try to dig a hole with a saw or to cut a board with a shovel.
5. The easiest route is not always shortest. The shortest route is not always best.
6. You are capable of astonishing things.
7. Be willing to admit when you're wrong.
8. You have the power to change your own story.
9. Always, always remember where you came from.
10. Experience is your greatest treasure.

Love,
Grandma Tulsia

297

I feel like a tent when you take out the poles, and I'm hoping someone will roll me up and put me in a bag and shove me in the closet until it's summertime again.

But then I remember telling Dad I was going to do something amazing tonight. I realize that I still can. It's just not going to be the same amazing thing I was planning on originally.

I shove my poles back into place and feel like myself again.

I have to go inside, I say.

Thank you both. for everything.

"You're welcome," says Emily, her eyes like a ladder to a safe, warm loft.

"Good luck," says Milton, his tiny fist extended in a gesture of brotherly support.

I give it a bump, take the folder and the book, and march toward the volcano that doesn't even know it's about to erupt.

When I get back to the group,
Hilly has just won a round of Simon
Says. Even the Dublingers are laughing.
It's a happy picnic,  and I'm about to

rain   all
                    over it.

I'd like to challenge for my Historian badge,
I say.

"My goodness," says Veronica. "I'm glad you're on such
a roll, but it's time to move on to tonight's lesson."
"I'm sorry," I say. "But this can't wait."
"No, really, Moxie—"

"I MEAN
IT,"

I say, the ice in my
voice stopping all the
ships in the harbor.

For a minute, Veronica and I have a staring contest
of our own, but then she says, "All right. I think
we have time for *one more* challenge."

My heart begins to pound. My wrists begin to sweat. I don't want to do what I have to do next.

I somehow find my feet and discover my voice and speak with my chin up and my back straight and as much of a flourish as I can manage at the moment, which is really not much of a flourish at all.

"The challenge is to discover and document an untold story of Tiddlywhump's past. I had a question about one of our town's most famous residents, so I went to the LOCAL HOUSE of HISTORY to look for the answer. But, strangely, the information I needed wasn't where it was supposed to be. Instead, I found it at the ... LIBRARY."

I hold up the folder. In an instant, Veronica's expression shifts from sheer surprise to towering fury to total despair. And then it goes flat, like mountains against the evening sky as the sun goes down. There's no emotion or fight, just a sense that a hurricane is coming and there's nowhere she can hide.

"Scouts, I think that's enough for tonight," says Veronica, and when everyone starts to protest, she says, "Sorry, but I'm suddenly not feeling well. Until your parents come, you can use the time to practice for your badges. Moxie, could you please help me clean up?"

I pick up the mixing bowls and empty eggshells and follow her into the kitchen, dragging my heart behind me like a thousand-pound weight.

Veronica takes a deep breath and leans against the island in the middle of the kitchen like it's taking all the strength she has to stay standing.

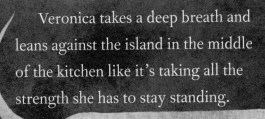

Where did you get that folder?

She's not accusing me. It's just a question.

I think you know. The question is, where did *you* get it?

I think you know.

We stand there looking at each other, knowing things we wish we didn't and neither having a clue what to do about it. Veronica takes the folder and pulls out the clipping.

So . . . you know I used to go by Ronnie. Is that why you're mad?

I've known *that* for a long time.

You have?

Yes, and it doesn't bother me.

It doesn't?

Not at all. I like the idea that you can change your own story. That's one of my favorite parts of the Credo. I used to be just an average elementary school student, but then I *decided* to become the world's greatest fourth-grade detective.

Veronica's face turns hopeful, like things are not as bad as she thought.

"But I also like the part about remembering where you came from. I, for one, used to be a funny-looking kindergartner with a unicorn ponytail! That's *my* experience. And my experience is *my* treasure!"

This isn't *your* treasure,

I say, holding up the letter.

This belongs to Julia.

Veronica says nothing. She stands there like a crumbling fortress as the catapults advance.

I can almost *halfway* understand someone borrowing someone else's good advice. But . . . borrowing someone else's *story*? Someone else's *accomplishments*?

I hold up

When in Rome

and suddenly Veronica stops looking like Veronica. She slouches. Her eyes are tired and unsure. She looks like . . .

Ronnie Collins.

She starts doing dishes and stares out the window. She starts to speak, but her voice has lost its punch.

I felt lost and out of place as a kid. I always loved that letter from my great-grandma. It seemed to hold all the secrets to the person I wanted to be.

And then she turns and looks me in the eye.

When I grew up, my dream was to inspire other girls the way she'd inspired me. But I figured no one would want to join a club run by a shy librarian named Ronnie. I needed a better story. So I read every book I could find until I discovered Constance Cavendish and instantly knew who I was meant to be. I loved this strong, smart woman's incredible adventures. So I borrowed a few.

How many?

I'm not sure. Once I started, it was hard to stop.

"Your adventures on the Mudflats of Mantú?"

"Volume Thirty-Four:  MANTÚRIAN CANDIDATE."

"The time you were named honorary queen of Bellingrad by taming the Piebald Jackal?"

"Volume Twenty-One: QUEEN ME."

"Saving seven orphans in a leaky kayak from plunging over the Fickle Falls of Far Fleggins?"

"Volume Eighteen: The HARDER THEY FALLS."

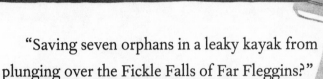

A **HORRIBLE** thought pops into my brain and tumbles right out of my mouth.

What about the Annabelle Adams books? You said you've never read them, but if you're a librarian who loves mystery and adventure, you must have, right?

I've read every book in the series seventeen times.

Why did you lie?

I've borrowed some stories from Annabelle, too. I just haven't been telling them since finding out you're such a big fan.

My heart is as dark and empty
as the clear night sky.

Veronica didn't travel the world solving puzzles and battling injustice—she made up a life that she borrowed from books. She didn't come up with timeless advice for the betterment of young women—she stole it from her great-grandma. She changed her story, all right, but then she forgot where she came from.

I want to cry and yell and throw a plate against the wall, all at the very same instant. Instead, I take off my sash and drop it in the garbage can along with the broken eggshells. My badges are nothing but colorful lies.

I pause in the doorway, wishing I could turn back time, searching every inch of my experience for a way to fix this problem.

I just have to ask: Was any of this *real*?

I look at Veronica with all my hope. This is the moment when the adult is supposed to pull out the perfect explanation that will make everything all right. I'm willing and ready to hear it. I'm waiting.

But Veronica says nothing at all. She looks at me as if I've just unplugged her heart from the battery that keeps it beating.

I turn to leave, but when I get to the door, I hear my fellow Scouts in the meeting room, joking and laughing and carrying on. None of them knows that everything is different now. And I'm not going to be the one to tell them.

I run out the back door and into the night and wait behind a bush until Dad comes to take me home again.

CHAPTER 18: TWO AND A HALF CONVERSATIONS

For the first time in weeks, my big brain is not busy thinking about badges, and so when Mr. Shine tells us about biomes and how an organism that thrives in one might not do so well in another, I actually sit there and listen. Which is such a shocking turn of events that, as soon as the recess bell rings, he calls me over to his desk.

What's wrong, Moxie?

Mr. Shine is a tantalizing swimming hole you can't help but jump into.

It's Veronica. She isn't who she said she was.

Mr. Shine gives me a long, sad look, but he doesn't gasp in horror or pound his fist in rage.

I talked to Ronnie after your meeting last night. She filled me in on everything.

Then why aren't you just as angry as I am?

Because she's my friend.
Because I can see both sides.

But she—

Mr. Shine looks me in the eye.

Can you count to ten in seven languages?

Yes, but—

Can you navigate unknown terrain using nothing but a compass and a map?

While that is true, I—

Did you boldly eat the eyeball of a trout?

I suddenly remember spending some time yesterday bragging to Mr. Shine about my trout eyeball heroics.

I absolutely did.

"And who is responsible for all that?"

"But . . . *Veronica didn't follow her own advice!*"

"That may be," says Mr. Shine. "But isn't it still very good advice? Aren't you glad you had the chance to learn it?"

"Are you saying something can be good for you *and* a lie at the *very same time?*"

Mr. Shine smiles a sad smile and says,

Weirdly . . . yes.

How is the world supposed to make a shred of sense when teachers say things like this?!

Mr. Shine, I appreciate your help, but it's **DEFINITELY** not HELPING.

I march out of the classroom to salvage the last few minutes of recess.

But instead of heading to the schoolyard, I find myself turning toward the main office, because what I need is a heart-to-heart with the noble, tough-talking pillar of wisdom and truth known as PRINCIPAL JONES.

But to reach her, I must somehow get past the FORBIDDING ARCHIPELAGO of VOLCANIC DESPAIR known as Mrs. Breath, who, as luck would have it, is on the telephone when I get to the main office, which means she cannot remind me that I am supposed to sit on the small, uncomfortable bench across from her desk while I patiently wait to see Principal Jones.

Which means I can *pretend* I forgot how this works and slide past Mrs. Breath like an explorer paddling on a piranha-infested river while an angry jaguar paces on the shoreline.

As the oven in Mrs. Breath's soul ignites with hot-white rage, I knock quietly on Principal Jones's door and slip inside when I hear her say, "Come in."

"Hello, Moxie," says Principal Jones, gesturing to the larger, less uncomfortable bench where kids sit to be yelled at or punished or occasionally consoled.

Principal Jones, this is the worst day of my life.

I see how this might sound like an exaggeration, so before Principal Jones can say, *It can't be as bad as you think*, I say, "And it really is as bad as I think." And before she can say, *Well then, tell me about it*, I say, "So I'm going to tell you about it."

All right, she says. I'm all ears.

As you probably know, I have recently joined the Wonder Scouts. But the awful truth is that my Scout leader made us believe she was one thing when she was something else entirely.

I look at Principal Jones and can tell that she is about to give me some wise advice, but before she can do it, I say,

Here's where you would tell me that what *really* matters is that she was *trying* to do the right thing, which is all anyone can ask, because life is so complicated.

And I would answer you by saying, yes, but she wasn't being *honest* with us.

And then you would look at me and pause for a second like you do when you want me to think extra hard about something.

Principal Jones looks at me like she does when she wants me to think extra hard.

And then I would realize that . . . *I* wasn't being entirely truthful with Veronica, *either*, and that I have my *own* apologizing to do.

Principal Jones looks as if she's watching the most exciting moments of an action movie.

313

And *then* you'd remind me that two people who have both made mistakes should try to find a way to forgive each other for the handful of *bad* things that have happened, before they throw away all the *good* things that came along with them.

Principal Jones is nodding, as if we are playing 20 Questions and I am very close to finding the answer.

Finally, you would tell me that you *believe in me* and are confident that, in the name of our noble mascot, Eddie the great horned owl, I have the wisdom, patience, and courage to do the right thing.

Principal Jones's eyes get wide, the way eyes do when someone is about to sneeze.

And because that would probably make me cry, you would offer me a tissue.

Principal Jones gestures to her box of tissues. I take one and blow my nose. But I do not cry. I am too busy figuring out what Principal Jones and I should do and say next.

314

Principal Jones looks at me like I'm a leaf blower that just showed up in the middle of her card game, and I realize I should probably stop standing on her bench.

Does that sound about right?

I ask, climbing down and folding my hands politely in my lap.

Principal Jones looks at me the way my mom might if she were here at this moment— WITH WONDER AND LOVE & MAYBE EVEN PRIDE.

I couldn't have said it better myself.

May I go now?

I think you definitely should. Especially since Mrs. Breath might get off the phone at any moment.

Principal Jones and I share a dignified nod. And then I open her door and sprint past Mrs. Breath's desk on legs that match the four-alarm tornado in my heart.

I race back down the hall to Mr. Shine's classroom just as the class is returning from recess.

I owe you an apology,

I say between great heaving breaths.

But I owe Veronica an even bigger one. Do you know where I can find her?

Mr. Shine smiles. "She lives in an apartment above the ice cream parlor. But," he says, realizing what I'm thinking, "she's heading to the airport sometime this afternoon."

That makes no sense! "Why would she go to the airport?"

Mr. Shine gives me a kind, sad smile. "She told me she had to go away for a while. But she wouldn't say where."

"Thanks," I say, taking my seat. I look at the clock. It's already 1:37 p.m. Veronica could be leaving *at this very moment*. But there is the unfortunate problem of school and the fact that it is not over.

I try my hardest to listen as Mr. Shine reads us a famous poem about having to choose between two paths in the woods and how the decision is tricky because one path is going to be much more challenging than the other, but also really important because they lead to very different places.

My brain is full of thoughts and questions that pop up one after another like those mechanical gophers you whack with a hammer at the carnival.

WHERE'S VERONICA GOING?

WHAT IF I DON'T GET TO TALK TO HER BEFORE SHE LEAVES?

WHAT CAN I SAY TO MAKE HER FORGIVE ME?

318

I distract myself by trying to answer the final question with a pencil and a piece of paper. When I'm done, I turn back to the other questions but find I have no answers.

If one path is doing nothing and the other is doing something that is difficult and against the rules but also extremely important, then there is no choice at all.

I raise my hand. "Excuse me, Mr. Shine. I have to go to the bathroom."

"Okay," he says in a way that makes me think he might be slightly suspicious of my motives.

But I do not stick around long enough to find out. Instead, I'm out the door, running down the hallway and out onto the sunny sidewalks of Tiddlywhump. It is a glorious day.

Eventually, I get to the ice cream parlor and see a set of side stairs I've never noticed before. I scamper up and peek through the window, and there is Veronica, putting a shirt in her suitcase.

I take a deep breath and knock.

When she opens the door, we stand there for a moment, not knowing what to do. Luckily, I remember the piece of paper in my pocket.

"Here," I say, handing it to her. "I'd like to challenge for my Scribe badge."

Veronica reads it out loud.

Dear Veronica,

REAL is a funny word. It means different things to different people.
I joined Wonder Scouts on a top secret undercover case. I didn't tell you my REAL reason for joining.
That fact about frog blood came from Annabelle Adams. So did the battery-gum-wrapper-fire-starting trick. Saying I came up with them myself was sneaky, and I'm sorry.
Julia is a big part of where you came from, for sure, but so is Constance. Maybe the stories you told us weren't REAL, but the lessons we learned from them sure are.
Maybe neither of us was being 100% REAL, but now I see I can't be mad at you without being mad at me, too. How about I forgive you and you forgive me and we go back to how things were?

Your REAL friend and fan,
Moxie McCoy

Veronica's eyes hover on the verge of tears.

Thank you, she says. That's one of the best essays I've ever read.

She reaches into her pouch and pulls out a SCRIBE BADGE.

"Which means you're going to need this," she says, opening a drawer and pulling out my sash.

It's a little bit eggy but otherwise okay.

"Thanks," I say, surprised at how relieved I am to have it back.

"Look closely," says Veronica. There, between Polyglot and Iron Gut, and just above Scientist, is a badge that wasn't there before.

"What you did last night—standing up to me like that—took more courage than I've ever seen from anyone, *including* my great-grandmother."

I run my fingers over the Intrepid badge.

I love it so much.

"And today, admitting *you* were wrong, too . . . that takes the kind of strength that muscles alone can't manage. And you surely earned this with your . . . *research* into my past."

She pulls out the Mighty and Historian badges and pins them to my sash.

"Do you know what this means?"

I look down. There may be 20 badges on my sash, but there shouldn't be. I take out my seam ripper and start to remove OBSCURE Facts!

I didn't really earn this one.

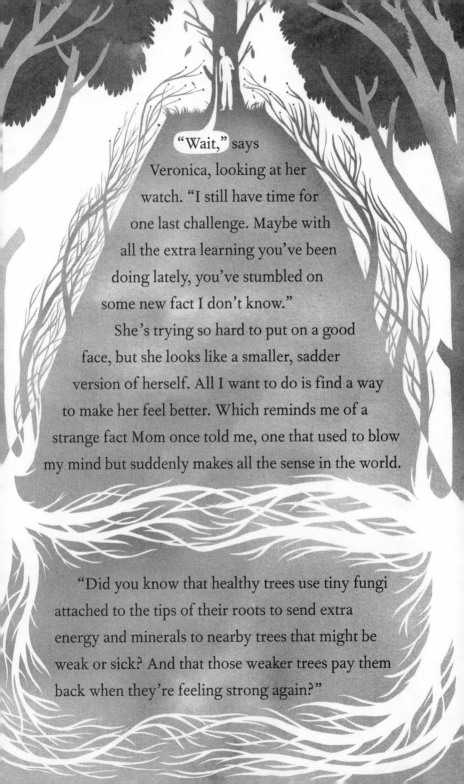

"Wait," says
Veronica, looking at her
watch. "I still have time for
one last challenge. Maybe with
all the extra learning you've been
doing lately, you've stumbled on
some new fact I don't know."

She's trying so hard to put on a good
face, but she looks like a smaller, sadder
version of herself. All I want to do is find a way
to make her feel better. Which reminds me of a
strange fact Mom once told me, one that used to blow
my mind but suddenly makes all the sense in the world.

"Did you know that healthy trees use tiny fungi
attached to the tips of their roots to send extra
energy and minerals to nearby trees that might be
weak or sick? And that those weaker trees pay them
back when they're feeling strong again?"

"Wow," says Veronica with a warm smile. "I had no idea. Sounds like I have a lot to learn from trees."

"I think you're doing just fine," I say. There is a pause like an ICICLE waiting to MELT when the winter sun pops out from behind a cloud.

Then she opens her arms and we have a hug that would probably win a prize on a planet with a shortage of regular sports.

When we're done, she looks taller and stronger and more like herself again.

This means you've done it, she says.

You're the first Wonder Scout to earn all twenty badges.

Thanks, I say, trying to sound as happy as I can. But getting badges seems like a small thing at the moment.

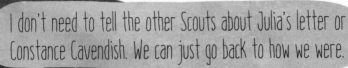

There's a question I have to ask. "Did you break into the Local House of History?"

Veronica smiles like it hurts a little. "When I heard about the Julia Wonder exhibit, I panicked and figured I'd better see what they knew about the real me. I'm ashamed to admit it, but, yes, I climbed in through a basement window one night. And got caught by someone working late."

"Solitary Historian Bernard Buxton?"

"Yes. Bernie is an . . . old friend. He'd called the police before he realized it was me, but when I explained that I was trying to make a new life, he let me keep my file and helped me slip out just before they arrived."

325

"Bernie . . . must be a pretty good guy."

"He really is."

My brain has the unpleasant experience of having to rewire itself by replacing a bad opinion of my nemesis with a slightly more generous one.

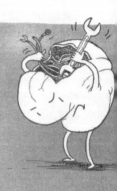

"I figured Wendell and Upchurch had stolen the file," I say. "To keep you from your share of Julia's inheritance."

Veronica's eyes get wide.

"You really *are* an

ACE DETECTIVE.

My cousins will never understand this, but the most valuable thing Julia left us isn't her riches. It's her incredible courage and heart. Wendell and Upchurch can keep Julia's money, and I will try harder to live up to her legacy."

Veronica pauses for a minute before lifting her compass from around her neck.

This is a treasure I didn't earn, so it isn't actually mine. But you, Moxie McCoy, know who you are. You're not afraid to admit when you're wrong. This compass belongs to *you*. I have to go find my own.

Veronica gives me a bittersweet smile and places the chain around my neck. The tears that didn't come earlier show up all of a sudden, but since there is no endless box of tissues here, I get Veronica's shirt good and wet instead.

Then the clouds clear and we're smiling again. I'm full of BURNING QUESTIONS.

Where are you going?

Italy! To see Saint Peter's Basilica for real. It's time for an actual adventure.

I'm excited for you, but . . . what about the Wonder Scouts? We *need* you. *I* need you. The Dublingers *desperately* need you! You're the only thing that's keeping them from being 100% horrible.

Veronica gives me an encouraging smile. "Don't worry. I've already found the perfect replacement."

"What? *Who?!*"

"I don't think you'll be disappointed," she says with a wink.

We hear a honk outside. Veronica's taxi is waiting.

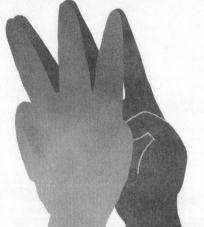

"Time to go," she says, picking up her suitcase.

"What about all this other stuff?" I ask. The room is still full of the sorts of things that people have.

Veronica looks around and gives a gentle sigh. "I don't need it anymore."

Suddenly, she looks like she's just put down the elephant that has been sitting on her shoulders. She has Veronica's strength and Ronnie's goofy smile. She's lighter and happier. She looks just like . . . herself.

I raise my three middle fingers in a *W*, and she does the same. We touch the tips together.

With that, she's out the door and into the cab and rolling

off

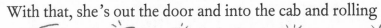

When she's gone, the room feels
different, like its heart is missing.

I clutch my compass and scamper down the stairs and
run back to school like an ostrich being chased by a cheetah.
As far as Mr. Shine knows, I have been in the bathroom a
really long time.

CHAPTER 19: THE WONDER GOES ON

You're never going to believe it!

says Milton, handing
me the morning paper.

**The Local House of History
needs an intern.**

The Local House
of History seeks a
Junior Historian
to help curate
exhibitions. Must
be hardworking,
organized, detail-
oriented, and
passionate about
Tiddlywhump.

Milton is excited. "It
would be the perfect job for me!"

But then he remembers. Milton is nothing
if not loyal.

"If only the Historian in Charge of No One hadn't
treated you so badly."

"Actually, I've heard from a reliable source that Soon-to-
Be Chief of Someone might not be *quite* as bad as I thought."

I tell Milton how Veronica got the missing file.

In that case, I think I'll apply,

he says with a grin.

You definitely should.

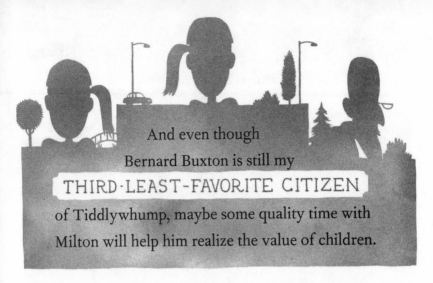

And even though
Bernard Buxton is still my
THIRD·LEAST-FAVORITE CITIZEN
of Tiddlywhump, maybe some quality time with
Milton will help him realize the value of children.

But Milton's gears are turning on something else now. "So that means Detective Multani never figured out the truth about what happened that night. I guess he isn't as great as we thought."

"He certainly isn't Tiddlywhump's finest," I say, feeling around in my sweatshirt pocket. The seam ripper is still there. I pick up my sash and remove the DETECTIVE BADGE.

YOU, Milton McCoy, I say, pinning it on his shirt, **YOU** are Tiddlywhump's finest.

What are you doing?

Milton is dismayed.

You earned this. There's no way I would have figured out what the Dublingers were up to without you.

But what about becoming the first Scout to earn all twenty badges? I thought that was the whole point?

The point of Wonder Scouts is learning things and having fun.

Milton places his tiny palm on my forehead.

Are you feeling okay?

I give him my biggest grin.

Never better. Plus, I'll probably earn another Detective badge by the end of the day. Because *I* am Tiddlywhump's *other* finest.

Milton rolls his eyes and smiles in relief to know I'm still the same old Moxie and haven't entirely lost my mind.

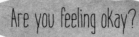

Our work is done. The case is closed. Calamity has been thwarted. For the moment, at least.

I spend the day thinking about Veronica.
Wondering what sort of adventures she's
having and treasures she's discovering and
stories she's collecting as she goes.

After dinner, Dad takes me to the community center.
We pull up to the curb, and there are the Dublingers,
doing their best imitation of a
barbed-wire fence

"Tracy. Tammy. I just want to offer a
'Thank you!'" I say it with all the cheer and
warmth and love my heart can hold. "I'm
extremely indebted to you both."
They glare at me with deepest suspicion.
It's clear that neither wants to speak
but both need to know what
they did to make me
so happy.

I intend to wait them out. About `30 SECONDS` pass before Tammy can't stand it anymore.

Thank us for *what?*

If you two hadn't spent so much time trying to keep each other from getting to twenty badges, I never could have . . . caught up.

I take off my coat with a flourish, revealing my

19 BADGES

The gasps that follow are as satisfying as a

DOUBLE-STUFFED BOSTON CREAM DONUT.

Isn't it neat that all three of us are tied?

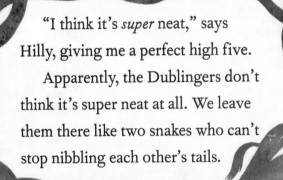

"I think it's *super* neat," says Hilly, giving me a perfect high five.

Apparently, the Dublingers don't think it's super neat at all. We leave them there like two snakes who can't stop nibbling each other's tails.

Everyone is chatting and joking around, waiting for the meeting to begin. I keep my eye on the door, but whoever is coming to lead us is late. Who could it be? Veronica left gigantic shoes to fill. Principal Jones would be a worthy replacement if only she weren't so busy with the single most important job in Tiddlywhump. But who else could possibly match up?

Just then I hear a familiar voice say,

Moxie.

And for a moment,
I think I must be
sound asleep and
dreaming.

Because suddenly there she is.

My magnificent mom, back from her adventure.

In this very room. At this very moment.

It might not be proper Scout protocol, but I give her the biggest hug and almost cry a little but instead, I just say, "Hi."

"Hi," she says with the special smile she uses only for me.

"You're *back*?" It's clear she's back, but it seems impossible.

"I'm back."

"But why didn't you . . . ?"

"I thought it would be a fun surprise."

"But what are you doing . . . *here*?"

"Mr. Shine asked Dad if he knew anyone who might want to lead the Wonder Scouts for a while. Turns out, he did."

"And you just *happened* to get home at the *exact moment* I needed you most?"

Mom smiles and rests her hand on my cheek and looks into my eyes like she's seeing a miracle happen. "That's kind of a mom specialty," she says with a wink.

I'm about to start crying in front of the Dublingers, which would be even worse than sharing a piece of caramel with them.

As I try to find words that fit the size of
the moment, Mom bends down and whispers,

I love you,

in my ear.

I whisper it back.

Then we both remember that we're here for a reason,
and we take our place in the circle.

Mom starts to speak.

Hello, Wonder Scouts! My name is
Maggie McCoy. I'm here to tell you
that Veronica was needed for some
important business and will be out of
the country for the foreseeable future.

Everyone stands there with wide eyes
and loud thoughts, not knowing what to say.

Fortunately, I just got back from my own adventure,
and so she asked if I might be willing to step in.

Where have you been?

asks Hilly.

And what have you been doing?

"I've been off the northeast coast of New Zealand," says Mom, "living in a submarine and researching supergiant amphipods. They share a common ancestor with land-based insects, so I wanted to understand how their habitat caused them to become something entirely different."

"Did you figure it out?" asks Henrietta.

"It's a work in progress," says Mom with a laugh.

"Over time, insects developed the parts they needed to live on land and amphipods developed the parts they needed to live in the deepest parts of the ocean. Every creature, from the shrimp to the antelope, has exactly the parts and characteristics it needs to thrive in its specific environment. The same is true for you guys. You grow and change with each new experience, learning the things you need to learn to be the best possible versions of yourselves."

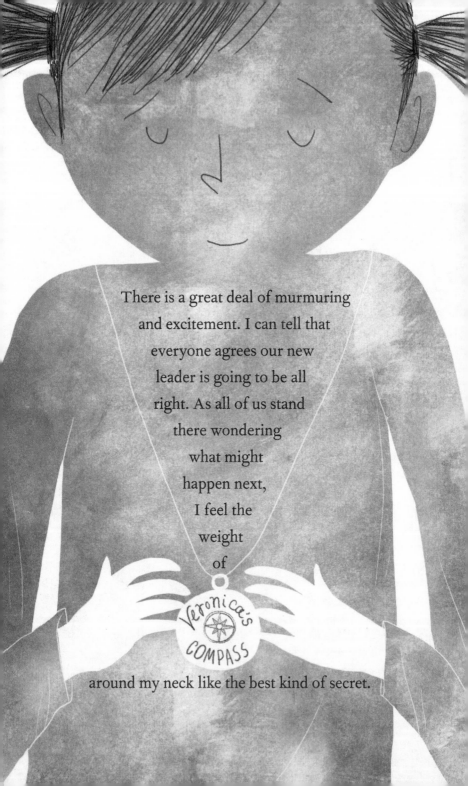

There is a great deal of murmuring and excitement. I can tell that everyone agrees our new leader is going to be all right. As all of us stand there wondering what might happen next, I feel the weight of Veronica's Compass around my neck like the best kind of secret.

As I open my mouth and start to sing, eleven other girls sing with me. We might be using the same words, but we each have different voices, different stories, different sets of experiences. We're each trying our best to be who we are and figure out who we will choose to become. And whether we sound perfect or terrible or somewhere in between, we are singing this song together.

I look around the circle and know exactly who I am.

There's no one else
I'd rather be.

SPREAD THE WONDER!

Veronica started Wonder Scouts to show the girls of Tiddlywhump that they can do anything. But anyone with an interest, passion, cause, goal, or dream can start their own club. Even you!

HERE'S HOW TO DO IT.

FIGURE OUT YOUR MISSION.

What do you want to accomplish or learn about or celebrate? Do you want to clean up a local park or abolish the marshmallow or teach every kid on your block how to ride a unicycle? Once you decide what you're trying to do, it's much easier to actually do it.

JUST SAY NO to MARSHMALLOWS

WRITE A CREDO.

Just as Julia advised in her letter, your credo says what you stand for and believe in. Things like *HONESTY*, *ADVENTURE*, curiosity, and *CHEESECAKE*, for example. Once you can say what you believe in, it's easier to find people who believe in the same thing (especially if it's cheesecake).

CHOOSE THE PERFECT NAME.

You can call your club Wonder Scouts if you want to (Veronica would be proud). But you could also call it

INVESTIGATOR club or STARGAZERS EXTRAORDINARY or AVOCADO AVENGERS.

Or anything else that sounds right to you. You can also design the perfect logo or badge if you want to.

YEAH! THUMBS UP!

WRITE A THEME SONG.

It's fun! You can write your own tune or use the tune of a song you already know and add your own words. Singing your theme song is a great way to start each meeting.

GET SOME ADULTS TO HELP.

I personally knew at least 4 dinosaurs when I was your age...

Adults are extremely old! Which means they know things. See if the adults in your life are willing to share what they've learned (the many kinds of dinosaurs) or the things they know how to do (changing the oil in a pick-up truck) with your club.

FIND MEMBERS!

Once you know your mission, your credo, and your name, write them on a piece of paper and hang it on the wall where people can see it. You'll have a club in no time. Here's the ad for the new club I'm starting.

WANTED!
MEMBERS for the
SMILING SLUG CLUB ™
I ♥ SLUGS
Dedicated to the admiration of the BEAUTIFUL, PERFECT, CHARISMATIC SLUG.
ALL ARE WELCOME *
* even Dublingers

MEET THE CREATORS

HELLO!

MATTHEW
ROBBI
ALDEN
JASPER
KATO
AUGIE

We are Matthew Swanson and Robbi Behr, and we made this book together. We are also married (to each other) and have four kids.

Matthew wrote the words and expressed his strong opinions about the illustrations. Robbi drew the illustrations, expressed her strong opinions about the words, and ignored most of Matthew's strong opinions about the illustrations.

Neither of us is a Wonder Scout, but if we were, neither would have as many badges as Tracy Dublinger.

Robbi would have her **Intrepid** badge because she is not afraid of anything (except Matthew's toenail clippings) and the **Iron Gut** because she will eat anything (except Matthew's toenail clippings), and she could win a **Staring Contest** against anyone and anything (except Matthew's toenail clippings).

Matthew does not have **Fire Starter** because Robbi won't let him touch matches or a flint or anything that is vaguely capable of creating a flame. Robbi doesn't have the **Master Baker**, because whenever she tries to make a meal, it takes four hours, tastes only sort of delicious, and makes a mess that takes a week to clean up.

Matthew would have SCRIBE because this is a book, and he WROTE IT.

Robbi would have MIGHTY because she just plain is.

Neither of us would have the **Pig Latin** badge ecausebay it'syay ickiertray anthay ouyay ightmay inkthay.

In conclusion, even both of us combined only have half as much moxie as Moxie.

WHAT'S THAT YOU SAY?

To get on our mailing list, browse our books, find our blog, or schedule us to speak at (or Skype with) your conference, library, or school, visit us at

WWW.ROBBIANDMATTHEW.COM.

Thanks for reading!

Matthew & Robbi